The CHRISTMAS TABLE

Also by Donna VanLiere

※

The
CHRISTMAS
TABLE

Donna VanLiere

ST. MARTIN'S PRESS

NEW YORK

First published in the United States by St. Martin's Press, an imprint of St. Martin's Publishing Group

www.stmartins.com

Library of Congress Cataloging-in-Publication Data

Names: VanLiere, Donna, 1966– author.
Title: The Christmas table / Donna VanLiere.
Description: First edition. | New York : St. Martin's Press, 2020. |
Identifiers: LCCN 2020028411 | ISBN 9781250164674 (hardcover) | ISBN
    9781250172495 (ebook)
Subjects: LCSH: Christmas stories.
Classification: LCC PS3622.A66 C485 2020 | DDC 813/.6—dc23
LC record available at https://lccn.loc.gov/2020028411

First Edition: 2020

10 9 8 7 6 5 4 3 2 1

For Troy,
who made our own kitchen and dining room tables
and inspired this book many years ago

The
CHRISTMAS
TABLE

ONE

May 1972

Thirty-five-year-old John Creighton pulls a slab of black walnut wood from the back of his pickup truck and carries it into the small workshop behind his home. He retrieves two more slabs, setting each one down on the worktable, sizing them up and his task at hand. What possibly made him think that he could build a kitchen table by October when the only other things he has made to this point are mirror and picture frames?

"So, this is the wood!"

He turns to see his thirty-year-old wife, Joan, standing in the doorway with her shoulder-length brown hair pulled back into a ponytail and holding their one-year-old son, Christopher. Their five-year-old daughter, Gigi, runs to her dad, wrapping an arm around one of his legs

1

and using the other hand to pound on the wood. "This is it!" he says. "Nice, isn't it?"

Joan runs a hand over the top of the wood, dusty and dirty from sitting in a farmer's barn on the outskirts of Elmore for years. "If you say so, I believe you." Christopher leans over in his mother's arms, and Joan lowers him so he can tap the wood with his chubby hand.

John reaches for a can of mineral spirits and swipes a cloth off the table behind him. He pours some of the mineral spirits onto the cloth and rubs it across a slab, revealing a handsome, rich, brown wood. "See that, Joansie! Beautiful!"

She smiles. "Remember John, you *don't* have to have this finished by October."

"I told you that we would not eat one more Thanksgiving or Christmas meal on that yellow Formica table, and you have my word," he says, saluting her.

"I'm just saying you don't have to rush it."

He leans against the workbench, looking at her. "Are you implying I won't be able to have it finished by October?" She opens her mouth. "Are you inferring you don't believe in my skills as a fine craftsman of tables? Are you saying I can't demonstrate my woodworking abilities on our local PBS affiliate?"

Joan laughs, setting Christopher down on the floor.

"I'm suggesting you've never made a table before, so take it easy on yourself."

John throws the white cloth on top of the wood. "Game on, sister! Game on! The table will be done, and it will be magnificent. The question is, will we be able to say the same about your turkey?"

"Are you calling yourself a turkey? Because that's how I interpreted that."

He rears his head back, laughing. "To be so pretty, you're a cruel woman, Joan Creighton."

She kisses his cheek, picks up Christopher, and reaches for her daughter's hand. "Dinner is in an hour and a half. I assume by your confidence that you'll be bringing the table in with you?"

John watches them leave. "You jest, but it could happen!" He turns to look at the wood, sighing and scratching his head. He walks back to his truck and opens the passenger-side door, then lifts several library books off the front seat. Carrying them back into the workshop, he stacks them next to the wood and picks up the first one filled with black-and-white photos of kitchen tables and other furniture pieces. He reaches for another book, titled *Measure Twice and Cut Once,* and opens the pages filled with step-by-step instructions for furniture projects. "Oh boy," he says beneath his breath. "Oh boy, oh boy, oh boy."

TWO

May 2012

Lauren Mabrey stands on the sidewalk at the entrance to Glory's Place, welcoming children as they arrive for the after-school program. She finished her shift in the floral department at Clauson's Supermarket an hour ago. Clauson's has given her the morning shift so she can be at Glory's Place each day by three to help. In November the twenty-three-year-old will mark two years of volunteering here and less than a year as a married woman. Just five months ago, in December, she stood in the gazebo in the heart of Grandon, surrounded by the townspeople who had adopted her as one of their own, and became Mrs. Travis Mabrey. She stumbled upon Grandon just a year and a half ago by accident, a literal crash. She was a witness to a car crash while driving through Grandon one day, was called back to town to identify the man involved in the hit-and-run, and never left. After years in foster families and with no family of her own to return to, she became a volunteer at Glory's Place, fell in love with the children at Glory's Place, with Grandon itself, and then with Travis.

Travis works with the Grandon Parks and Recreation Department, keeping ball fields in shape and the city's playground equipment safe. He mows the grass at city parks, paints and cares for the gazebo in the town square, and even places the giant star atop it for Christmas. They live in the house Travis bought two years ago, a small two-bedroom ranch that was built in the 1960s. Although Lauren would like to say that she has added a female's touch to the home, decorating has never been her strong suit. Part of her thinks it's because she moved from one foster home to the next and never really had it modeled for her, but the other part believes it's because she simply does not have an eye for it. Either way, their home still lacks warmth in color and feel, like Miss Glory's home or Dalton and Heddy's or Miriam's, and she wants to do something about it.

Her stomach feels queasy, and Lauren leans against the door, waiting for another wave of children to arrive. A knock on the glass of the door makes her jump. "What is wrong with you?" She turns to see Miriam looking at her from inside. Her colored strawberry-blond hair hangs just below her chin in a sleek bob and her pink oxford shirt is tucked impeccably into blue trousers on Miriam's trim frame. Her English accent and appearance would make anyone believe that she is demure, fragile even, but this isn't the Miriam that Lauren has come to love.

"Are you ill?" Miriam says, opening the door and sizing up Lauren. "You look dreadful."

Lauren shakes her head. "I ate sushi at work yesterday for lunch and it's been a rough two days."

Miriam groans. "Supermarket sushi! Do people really have to be told not to eat that? Isn't that akin to squirting cheese out of a machine onto nachos in a petrol station?"

"No! Clauson's has wonderful sushi. It's always fresh."

"And toxic," Miriam says. "Fresh and toxic. A wonderful combination." She looks at Lauren. "I'll finish here. Why don't you go inside and sit down or throw up or . . . whatever? One of Gloria's friends is coming in today for training and since I don't necessarily care to be around people, I will leave her training to you."

Lauren smiles. Miriam can pretend all she wants, but Lauren knows how much she loves these children and the work that is done at Glory's Place. Miriam loathes the thought that she's old enough to be a grandmother to most of the volunteers, but she loves them and the children here with the fierce, protective love of any grandma. It was Miriam who bought her wedding dress and it was Miriam who wrapped her arms around her when Lauren gave the dress to a young woman who couldn't afford a wedding gown of her own. Her bond to Miriam, Gloria, Stacy, and Heddy and Dalton here at Glory's Place is stronger than any she ever imagined having with any adult as a child growing up and she feels safe in a way she never thought possible.

The tutoring section of Glory's Place is behind a door and Lauren spends the next few minutes here, sitting quietly at a desk and hoping this queasiness doesn't blow up into food poisoning. She pops a couple of peppermint candies into her mouth, something that Heddy told her would help ease nausea, and lays her head on the desk in front of her. She stays here for several minutes until she hears Gloria's voice inside the big room. Gloria *is* Glory's Place; it was her idea many years ago to help single moms and struggling families and that morphed into an after-school program that's open year-round. Lauren opens the door and sees Gloria standing in the middle of the big room with her arms open wide.

"This is the best day because all of you are here with us," Gloria says in her Southern accent that sounds like a big, vocal hug. She says this every day to the children, many who come from broken homes and some who are in the foster care system, like Maddie once was before Amy, a volunteer, and her husband, Gabe, adopted her.

More than thirty children from the ages of five to thirteen look on as Gloria, or "Miss Glory" to them, welcomes them. Her salt-and-pepper curls have been pulled back hastily with a clip she keeps in the top drawer of her desk and she's wearing a Betty's Bakery T-shirt. She and Miriam could not be less alike, but they are the best of friends. "I have a friend of mine who is going to be volunteering with us and I'd like all of you to meet her. I met Andrea and her husband, Bill, a few years ago, and she has been a wonderful friend to me, and I know she will be a wonderful friend to you, too. She's helped from time to time over the years, but now wants to help more, and we can always use more hands around here. Say hi to Mrs. King."

The children shout out hellos and Andrea waves. She looks to be in her forties, is petite but slightly pudgy with a big smile and warm, blue eyes and short brown hair. She looks like a woman who is easy to be with and even easier to hug. "Call me Miss Andrea," she says. "I can't wait to get to meet all of you. I always wanted to help more at Glory's Place, but couldn't do it a lot because I often traveled with my job and was so busy with raising my kids, but now they're both practically grown so I'm excited to be helping and meeting all of you!"

Gloria claps her hands together. "All right, if you're supposed to be in tutoring, then you know the way there.

If you're supposed to be reading with Stacy, you know where to go, or if you're outside with Dalton, then head that way." She swings an arm around like she's about to pitch a fastball. "Let's make it a great day!" The children begin to scatter and Gloria waves when she sees Lauren. "This is Lauren," she says to Andrea.

Lauren sticks out her hand to Andrea. "So nice to meet you. I'll be training you today."

Gloria puts an arm around Lauren's shoulder. "Lauren is one of my favorite people in the whole world and so is her new husband, Travis." She looks at Lauren. "And Andrea is also one of my favorite people in the world. Just don't tell Miriam I said that because I never include Miriam as one of my favorite people in the world."

"I heard that, Gloria!" Miriam bellows from across the room. "You are boorish and ill-mannered."

"And she wonders why she isn't one of my favorite people," Gloria whispers as she turns to walk to Miriam.

"They've always been like that, right?" Andrea says, watching Gloria and Miriam quibble.

Lauren laughs. "As long as I've known them. But if you listen really close you can hear how much they love each other. They're the best of friends. I want to have a Gloria or Miriam when I'm their age." Lauren turns and walks to the door behind them. "What brings you to help here?" she asks, opening the tutoring door.

"Well, like I said, my kids are grown or nearly grown, and I have more time on my hands these days."

"How many kids do you have?" Lauren says, closing the door behind them.

"Two. A boy and a girl. My daughter is in college and my son is a senior in high school." Andrea watches as an older woman with dark almond skin leans over a child around ten and points to something in a book in front of him.

"That's Heddy," Lauren whispers. "She and Dalton have been here since the beginning with Gloria and Miriam. And that's Amy over there. She and Gabe got married on the same day that Travis and I did, and they adopted Maddie, one of the children from here." She signals for Andrea to follow her to the door and is quiet as she opens it, stepping into the big room again.

"There are usually two volunteers in the tutoring room at a time and we help with homework."

Andrea smirks at the thought. "I don't think I'd be able to offer much help. How they do things in school now is so different from when I was a child."

"We all thought that when we started helping with homework, but everybody has their strengths and we all just pitch in and . . ." She stops talking and puts her hand on her stomach.

"Are you okay?" Andrea says, concerned.

"Yes. I'm afraid my husband and I ate some bad sushi yesterday."

"He's sick, too?" Andrea asks.

Lauren shakes her head. "No. Just me. Didn't agree with me, I guess. It's made me so nauseous."

"And you're the only one nauseous?"

Lauren nods, exhaling as if that will blow the queasiness away. "Yeah. Isn't that strange?"

Andrea smiles. "Not really."

THREE

May 1972

Joan retrieves a stack of recipe cards from a drawer in the kitchen and sits down at the Formica kitchen table. Her mother handed these cards to her just weeks before her wedding to John. "If you can follow the steps of a recipe," her mom said, "you can make anything." Joan's trouble was following the steps; she usually managed to make a blunder and the recipe never turned out like her mom's. Her mom, Alice, had written down her favorite tried-and-true recipes and the ones that Joan loved the most as a child growing up. Joan wanted to be a good cook like her mom but had resorted to quick and easy meals each evening. She thumbs through the recipe cards, thinking that if John is determined to make a beautiful table for the holiday season, then she is also determined to put a beautiful meal on it. She stops at a card that reads "Hummingbird Cake." She used to love it when her mom made this cake but has been afraid to try it on her own, reasoning there are too many ingredients. She scans over them, reading her mom's notes beside some of the ingredients:

3 large, room-temperature eggs. Put them in some warm water for a few minutes if they're right out of the fridge.

2 teaspoons vanilla. Pay the extra money for the real stuff!

4 to 6 bananas. Roast them in the oven for best flavor! And keep the peels on! You need two cups.

1 cup pineapple. Buy a fresh one. Don't waste your time with that canned stuff!

2 cups roasted pecans. Let them roast a few minutes in the oven to bring out their best flavor! One cup is for the frosting.

Joan groans looking at all the extra steps her mother did: roasting bananas and pecans and cutting a fresh pineapple! She walks to the phone on the kitchen wall and dials her mom's number. "Mom! I'm going to make a hummingbird cake today."

"Really? Is it the recipe I gave you?" Alice asks.

Joan can imagine the excitement her mother must feel right now. Joan has never been anything close to the cook that her mother is and has rarely shown an interest in cooking. "Yep, your recipe, but good grief! Is all this roasting really going to make that big of a difference?"

"I don't know what it is, but there's something about adding just a little bit of heat to those bananas and pecans that brings out the best flavor!"

Joan sighs. She's stuck with roasting. "I've never even bought a pineapple in my life, let alone cut one" she says. Her mom laughs, talks her through it, and then says, "Can I talk with my grandbabies?"

Joan leans down, looking at Christopher. "You don't want a hummingbird cake for dessert, do you?" she asks, handing him the phone.

"I do!" Gigi says, making the toy car she's been playing with fly through the air. "If hummingbirds love it, then I will, too!"

"Then you'll help me make it?"

Gigi leaps into the air, holding the car like a rocket ship. "Yes!"

Joan chuckles. "Then say hello to Grandma and let's go to the grocery store. We've got a lot of things to buy."

May 2012

Heddy Gregory sits at a wooden desk with its too-worn top etched with jagged scars and stained with blotches of purple-black ink, and fills out paperwork for a new child at Glory's Place. This is the same paperwork and the same desk she has used year after year, but today when she presses a ballpoint pen down onto the information sheet, a leg on the desk collapses, making Heddy and the mother of the child gasp together. "Oh, my word!" Heddy says, grabbing the pictures of the children on top of the desk before they fall but letting the cup of pens crash to the floor.

Gloria pops her head out of her office at the commotion. "What's going on?"

"Apparently Dalton did not fix this leg!"

Hearing his name, Dalton walks across the big room and looks at the desk. "What'd you do, Heddy?" he says, winking at Gloria.

"The question is, what *didn't* you do?" Heddy says, leading the mother into the office to finish the paperwork.

"There's not much that I can do for this leg," Dalton says to Gloria. "It needs a new one. Do you want me to get it to Larry?"

Gloria shakes her head. "Larry would charge us twice what we paid for it."

"What did you pay for it?"

"Nothing. We got it out of Miriam's garage when we first opened, and it was a piece of junk then. Let's just get it out of here and one of us can get over to Larry's to see if he has anything we can buy. This space looks awfully big and boring without a table or desk here." She looks up and notices Lauren chatting with a child on the sidewalk and pats Dalton on the shoulder. "I'll grab Lauren to help get it out of here."

Dalton and Lauren load the desk into the back of Dalton's pickup truck as Gloria gives instructions to Lauren. "Just find something simple and nice at Larry's," she says. "Anything with a top and four legs would be nicer than what we've been using."

"I don't think I should be in charge of finding a new piece of furniture," Lauren says. "I can't even pick furniture out for our house."

"Oh yes you can!" Gloria says, leading her back into Glory's Place. "Larry can help. He knows the size space that we have, and he knows our budget."

"What is our budget?" Lauren asks.

"What is our budget, Dalton?" Gloria says.

"I have about forty dollars in my wallet," he says, grinning.

"And that's about what I have," Gloria says. "I bet Miriam has another forty, so let's say a hundred and twenty dollars."

Lauren steps into the bathroom before making the trip to Larry's. It's been five days since she ate the sushi from Clauson's and she still doesn't feel well. She knows now that it obviously isn't food poisoning but rather a virus. "Hi, Andrea!" she says when she exits the bathroom and sees Andrea across the big room.

"Lauren!" Andrea watches as Lauren slings her purse over her shoulder. "Are you leaving?"

"I'm headed to Larry Maccabee's to find a table or desk for the front entryway." She sits on a chair in the reading section and sighs, trying to catch her breath.

Andrea sits next to her. "Are you still not feeling well?"

"Just tired right now. It comes over me at weird times. I heard somebody at Clauson's talking about a virus going around."

"Still nauseous?" Lauren nods. Andrea looks up at the bathroom door. "And going to the bathroom more frequently?"

Lauren's brows rise and her eyes widen. "Yes! So frustrating."

Andrea pats her knee. "Tell you what, why don't I go to Larry's and you go to the doctor?"

"I can't do that to Miss Glory. She needs every volunteer once the kids arrive."

"Gloria wouldn't want any of us to be sick around the children, and Miriam said that Gabe is coming in with

Amy today, so we already have an extra person to cover for you."

Lauren nods. "Do you know Larry?"

Andrea smiles. "No, but I will after I get to his shop."

"Don't tell Gloria that I'm sick. I don't want her to worry."

"I won't say a word until you and your husband both know what's happening." Andrea smiles, watching Lauren walk across the big room and leave the building.

Larry Maccabee creates a mini dust storm inside his shop as he uses a power sander to lift years of polyurethane and what looks like nail polish abuse from a tabletop. He's had it for years in his workshop in hopes of restoring and reselling it but has never gotten around to it. The table was set aside and quickly became a catchall for extra tools, cans of stain, books and manuals, paintbrushes, and anything else that was in Larry's hand.

"Excuse me." His back is to the door, and Andrea knows there's no way he's going to hear her over that blasted sander. She spots the light switch and walks to it, flicking it on and off a couple of times. He spins around, turns off the sander, and pulls the earmuffs down around his neck. "So sorry to bother you," she says. "I didn't want to scare you because your back was to the door."

"I normally keep the door locked when I'm working with the power tools," he says, setting down the power sander and wiping sawdust from his forearms as he walks through his shop filled with a table saw, drill press, band saw, jointer, workbenches, belt sander, planers, clamps, and various hand tools hanging on each wall. Larry mills his own wood and has been making or refurbishing furniture for decades. He looks to be in his late sixties or early seventies with a crown of grayish brown hair, black-framed glasses, and a gently worn face. "How can I help you?"

"I'm Andrea King, and I'm looking for a table or desk for the entryway to Glory's Place. She said you'd know the size that would be best for that space."

"Sure! My wife, Melanie, and I were there when volunteers were cleaning and painting and getting Glory's Place ready."

Andrea looks around the shop, wondering what he has that might work. "Well, we've all pitched in and we have a hundred and sixty dollars to buy something. What do you have?"

"The one I was working on when you came in would be the perfect size but . . ." He glances up at it. "No. It's round. You need a rectangle." He moves to the side of the shop with a few pieces of finished furniture, and Andrea follows.

"I love the smell of a wood shop," she says. "It—"

"I do, too! Always have." He stands in front of two desks and taps one.

Andrea notices the price—$1,600. The one next to it is $1,200. "Beautiful work, Larry."

"That one there was a black walnut tree out at the Hurley farm. It had to be over a hundred years old and—"

Andrea lifts her hand. Gloria warned her that Larry would give the history of each project beginning with the tree when it was just a sapling. "It's beautiful, but we can't afford either of these desks. They are too much desk for what Glory's Place needs. Do you have anything else?" He shrugs and leads her to two more desks, one that has obviously been created by Larry with a price tag of $700 and the other a simple oak desk with single drawer that costs $350. "This one's nice and simple."

"It's an old library table I refinished," he says.

"It's really nice," she says, looking underneath the table.

He bends over to look as well. "What are you looking for under there?"

"I have no idea, but it feels like I should do this."

He shakes his head, chuckling. "When you're done looking under the hood, we can talk business."

"I think it will work great. Would you be able to take—"

"If Gloria needs it. Gloria can have it. I'm happy to donate it."

"That's awfully kind, Larry. Gloria said you're one of her favorite people."

"Ah," he says, making a growling sound in back of his throat. "She doesn't get out much."

FOUR

May 1972

J oan holds the recipe card in front of her and turns on the oven, preheating it to 350 degrees. She places four bananas in their peels on a cookie sheet and pours two and a half cups of pecans into a shallow baking dish. While she waits for the oven to reach the proper temperature, she takes the pineapple from the grocery sack and stares at it, then grabs a large knife from the drawer. She whacks off the top and then the bottom and goes to work on the sides, just as her mom instructed, each time realizing she needs to cut away more of the skin in order to remove what Gigi calls "the prickles." She cuts off a piece for the little girl.

"What is this again?" Gigi says, observing the moist yellow fruit in her hand.

"Pineapple," Joan says, handing a piece to Christopher.

"Mmm," Gigi says with her mouth full. "Good apple pie."

"Pineapple," Joan says, chuckling. She quarters the pineapple and cuts it into small chunks, enough for one cup. "I can't believe I'm putting bananas in the oven, but here we go!" She places the bananas and pecans inside the oven and closes the door, setting her timer for ten minutes. "The peels need to be black, and the pecans need to be getting darker and smell fragrant," Joan reads aloud from the recipe card.

"What's 'fabrant'?" Gigi asks, squatting down to look inside the oven.

"Fragrant," Joan says, reaching over and scratching the little girl's back. "It means they should smell good. Ready to mix everything together?" Gigi nods and Joan stands up. "Let's do it!" She smacks the countertop and moves to the refrigerator. "I totally forgot to put the eggs out. Okay, we'll put them in some water." She hands three eggs to Gigi and fills a bowl with lukewarm water. "Put them right in here."

"Why?"

"Because Grandma says so. If the eggs aren't at room temperature you can put them inside a cup of warm water for a few minutes."

"Why?" Gigi asks, filling a cup too full of water.

"Because Grandma says the eggs shouldn't be really cold when you're making a cake. They should be room temperature." Joan peers again at the recipe. "Okay, you can hold the sifter and I will put flour, baking soda, cinnamon, and . . ." She reads the recipe again to make sure she's grabbing everything. "Salt!" She measures each ingredient into the sifter and helps Gigi hold it while she turns the handle, sifting the ingredients into a bowl. "So far, so good!" Joan says, reassuring herself. When she smells the pecans, she opens the oven door and gives them a quick stir before closing it again.

"The bee-annas look bad," Gigi says, pointing.

"According to Grandma, that will make them taste really yummy." Joan combines the eggs and the sugar, and Gigi stirs the mixture as Joan adds the oil and vanilla. Reading from the card again, Joan pulls out a potato masher from a drawer and begins mashing the pineapple.

Gigi reaches for another piece. "I love this apple pie!"

Joan laughs. "Pineapple!" She adds the crushed pineapple to the batter and when the timer goes off, she runs to the oven, pulling out the pecans. "Ugh. They look too dark." She sighs. "Please don't be ruined." She sets the timer for another five minutes for the bananas.

"Who are you talking to, Mommy?"

"The pecans."

"I don't think they can hear you."

Joan sets the pan down on a hot pad, laughing. "Well, if they can, I'm hoping they will cooperate." She stirs the batter just until everything is incorporated; she is sure not to overstir, just as her mother cautioned on the recipe. After pouring some pecans into the top of the nut grinder, she lets Gigi turn the handle. Christopher reaches up, wanting to help, and Gigi sets the grinder on the floor in front of him so he can turn the handle, too.

"He can't do it," Gigi says, disappointed or flabbergasted at her brother.

"Put your hand on top of his," Joan says, pulling the bananas from the oven. "This just seems so wrong to do to these. They're black." She uses a knife and fork to open the peels and then scoops the mushy bananas into a bowl, where she mashes them with the potato masher. In order to complete the batter, Joan asks if she can finish crushing the pecans and takes the nut crusher from Gigi and Christopher, making him cry. She adds the bananas and one cup of the nuts to the batter and stirs it with a spatula.

"Looks like vomit," Gigi says, squinching up her face.

Joan agrees but knows if she says it out loud that Gigi will never try a bite. "Oh, this is just part of this cake's walk. Wait till you see what the cake looks like at the end of its journey!" Joan lifts the recipe card again, realizes she forgot to prepare the pans, and groans, wondering if she'll ever get the hang of cooking.

May 2012

Lauren waits inside the small patient room at the walk-in clinic and flips through the same magazine she's been reading for the last thirty minutes. When she hears someone opening the door, she looks up to see Debra, the physician assistant who was helping her earlier. "Your urine test results came back," Debra says, leaning up against the exam table, smiling. "You're pregnant."

Lauren's face drops. "What?"

"Pregnant."

"Pregnant." Lauren says the word as if she's trying to pronounce it for the first time.

"Is this good news?"

Lauren shakes her head as if rattling it so an answer will spill out. "I guess! I mean, yes! We just didn't plan it." She looks down at the floor and back up at Debra. "I thought it was food poisoning! Then I thought I had a virus! Did you suspect that I was pregnant when I came in here?"

Debra chuckles. "Do you know how many women I've asked if there's any chance they're pregnant who have said, just like you, 'Nope. Not possible'? With the kind of symptoms you had, I knew it was a good possibility, but we always need to make sure."

Lauren leans her head back against the wall. "I actually think Andrea knew before me!"

"Who's Andrea?"

"A woman I just met a few days ago. She must think I'm a dope."

Debra laughs and hands Lauren a prescription for prenatal vitamins. "If you don't have an ob-gyn, I can recommend some for you."

Lauren looks down at the prescription. She's pregnant. There's a baby growing inside of her, and she's her mother. Or his mother! The thought terrifies and exhilarates her as she slips the prescription into her purse.

FIVE

May 2012

Travis is using a Weed Eater around each pine tree that was planted in October on the edge of the Grandon ball fields. He's wearing the tan pants and navy shirt with the sleeves rolled up that the parks department employees wear, and he has a Grandon Parks Department ball cap pulled over his short-cropped brown hair. Earphones prevent his hearing Lauren's car in the parking lot behind him. She walks through the grass toward the row of pines and stands for a moment, watching him work. Travis has a sense of fun and wonder that she lacks and is kind with an easy way about him. She smiles, thinking about him; this baby will have the best father in all of Grandon. As he moves to the other side of the tree, Travis spots Lauren and turns off the Weed Eater.

"Hey!" he says, pulling off the earphones. "What are you doing out here?"

Grass is clinging to the bottom of each pant leg and bits of grass cover his forearms and hands; his face is wet with sweat, and he runs the palm of his hand across his forehead. Lauren smiles looking at him, thinking him the most handsome man she's ever met. "You're awfully cute covered in grass."

"Then you should go see Tim over on field eight. I bet he's absolutely adorable right about now," he says. She laughs, reaching into her purse. "So, what's up?" Travis says. "I thought you were at Glory's Place this afternoon."

"Well, I was, but I thought you should see this." She hands him the prescription, waiting.

He looks at it and up at her. "What is this?"

She smiles. "It's the name of a prenatal vitamin the doctor wants me to start taking."

"A prenat . . ." He looks down at the prescription again and then to her face. "You're pregnant?"

She shrugs. "It's definitely not a virus!"

Travis lifts the Weed Eater into the air, whooping as he does. "I'm gonna be a dad!" he yells for all the pine trees to hear. He grabs Lauren and lifts her off her feet, swinging her around and kissing her as she laughs.

Setting her down, he yells across the ball fields. "Hey, Tim! I'm gonna be a dad!"

"What?" Tim shouts, cupping his hand to his ear.

"I'm gonna be a dad!" Travis hollers back.

"I don't have it," Tim shouts. "It's back at the shed."

Lauren and Travis laugh, and he kisses her forehead. "So, when will the baby be here?"

"In December. A Christmas wedding and now a Christmas baby." Her eyes open wide at the thought. "Travis! We aren't ready for a baby! Our extra bedroom is filled with junk and we don't even have a kitchen table to eat off of!"

He puts his hands on her shoulders. "Then we will get rid of the junk in the spare bedroom and we will buy a kitchen table. Done. Nothing to worry about." He kisses her forehead again. "You are one hot mama! Do you know that?"

She shakes her head, walking toward her car. "I can't even with that," she says over her shoulder.

"Sexiest mom in Grandon!"

"That just sounds wrong!" she says, opening the car door.

"Own it!" he yells, loud enough for her to hear inside the car. She shakes her head, backing out of the spot. "I love you!"

She rolls down the passenger-side window and says, "I love you, too, my baby daddy!"

May 1972

John Creighton taps a nail through a long, narrow piece of plywood and barely taps the nail down into the top of the black walnut slabs he glued together two days ago. "Don't botch this," he mutters beneath his breath. Using the jig, he holds a pencil at the side of the plywood and slowly turns the jig around the top of the wood, drawing a seventy-degree circle. He breathes a sigh of relief when he sees that the circle is just the size he had determined. Picking up a woodworking book on the workbench behind him, he reads once again how to use the router to cut out this circle. He puts his earmuffs and safety goggles on as he reaches for the router. "Really don't botch *this*," he says, leaning over his work.

Inside their home, Joan pats dry a whole chicken, bending over and reading her mother's recipe as she does. The hummingbird cake fell slightly on top; she took it out too early, but John raved about it. He ate two pieces the night she served it, teasing her that he hoped she would love him when he gained an additional thirty pounds. When no one was looking, she had a few bites of what was left of the cake this morning for breakfast.

She reads her mother's writing: *Sprinkle salt and pepper inside the cavity and over the chicken. Cut up three tablespoons of butter and put it inside. Cut up another three tablespoons of butter and place it around the outside of the chicken.* Joan does as instructed and uses a paper towel to wipe the butter from her hands. She peels the skin from a clove of garlic and puts it inside the chicken, along with half a lemon and a chopped stalk of celery with its leaves. Having placed the chicken inside the preheated oven, she sets the timer for an hour and fifteen minutes and picks up the second recipe, this one for rosemary-parmesan potatoes.

These are so good with roasted chicken! Her mother wrote beneath their name on the card. *Remember how many you would eat? Always make extra!* Joan looks at the ingredients:

1 to 1½ pounds of new potatoes. Red potatoes work, too.

3 tablespoons vegetable oil

1 tablespoon fresh rosemary. Don't use the dried stuff in a jar!

2 to 3 tablespoons grated parmesan cheese. Yes, buy a wedge and grate it!

Joan cuts the potatoes in half and mixes them with all the ingredients, sprinkling a little salt and pepper on top of them. "They look yummy," she says, lecturing herself again for not learning how to cook before now.

May 2012

Lauren steps inside Glory's Place and notices that Gloria, Miriam, Andrea, Heddy, Stacy, and Amy are looking at Gloria's computer inside her office. She peeks her head into the room and Gloria looks over the top of the computer at her. "Come on in, babe. We're looking at some of the pictures for the new website."

Without Lauren realizing it, the words tumble out of her mouth. "I'm pregnant."

As if on cue, the six women look up at her at the same time, letting her words register with them. "What?!" Gloria says, sliding her chair back and running with her arms open to the ceiling toward Lauren with the other women following behind. "Did you just find out? Does Travis know? You didn't tell us before him, did you? That would never do. If you didn't tell him, we'll just pretend we don't know."

"He knows!" Lauren says, laughing.

"Oh, that's good!" Miriam says. "The father can get awfully offended if someone knows he's about to be a dad before he does."

"Well, I wasn't offended, but you can imagine my

surprise when someone else knew that I was pregnant before I even knew," Lauren says, grinning.

"The doctor?" Stacy says.

Lauren shakes her head. "No. Andrea." She points her finger at Andrea, laughing. "You knew!"

Andrea smiles. "I suspected. That's all."

"When are you due?" Gloria asks, both of her hands resting on the backs of Lauren's shoulders.

"Sometime in December, but I don't know a date! I have to find an obstetrician!"

"And we have to plan a baby shower," Heddy says.

"But before that we simply have to do something with Lauren's home," Miriam says. "A little color to make one realize they're not part of a lab experiment when walking through the front door, and a kitchen table is definitely in order, and a crib inside a nursery. And we simply must hang some things on the wall so the baby doesn't cry out in boredom from the plainness of it all."

Gloria shakes her head. "There are days when I think, 'Today's the day. Miriam won't blurt out whatever is on the top of her head. Today Miriam's brain will have a filter.' But then you say things like that, proving me wrong . . . again."

Miriam opens her mouth to defend herself when Lauren lifts hands, laughing. "It's okay, Gloria. I agree with everything Miriam said." Miriam gives Gloria a smug smile. "I've been wanting to do things with the house, but I just don't know what. Now that we know a baby is coming, I definitely want to make it more homey."

"Then I'm on it!" Miriam says, thrusting her index finger into the air.

Gloria sighs. "Those are the most chilling words that Miriam could say to anyone: *I'm on it!* Oh the terror of it all!"

SIX

May 1972

D on't let it get to soft ball," Joan's mother, Alice, says. Joan sighs on the other end of the phone. "What exactly does that mean? The recipe says to get it to soft-ball, but you say *don't* let it get to softball. Why do they call it softball anyway?"

Her mom chuckles. "It's not softball, like the sport. It's soft ball. It starts at 234 degrees. But don't let it get to 234. Take it off the burner when the thermometer gets to 233."

Joan stares at the thermometer in her hand with red liquid in the bottom that will climb up through the thermometer as the temperature rises. "My thermometer doesn't say 233. It just says softball." She catches herself. "Soft ball."

"Just take it off the burner before it reaches soft ball," her mother says. "You can also test a little bit of it by pouring it into some cold water. If it forms a soft ball in your hand, you know that it's ready."

Shaking her head, Joan says, "There's no way I'm trying that. I don't even know what that really means. Well, if anything, we can pour this over ice cream and eat it."

"You can do it!" Alice says. "I bet you'll all love it so much that you'll end up making another batch in a few weeks."

"We love Aunt DeeDee's fudge, Mom," Joan says, reaching for a pot. "It could be an entirely different story when *I* make Aunt DeeDee's fudge."

"Call me later and tell me how it turned out."

Joan hangs up the phone and puts the sugar into the pot with the milk. She then measures out a cup of Marshmallow Fluff and puts that into a separate small bowl, along with a cup of peanut butter. After she stirs the milk and sugar together, she turns on the burner and places the thermometer on the side of the pot so the bottom of it is immersed into the mixture. She is paranoid as she watches the temperature, stirring consistently as the red moves upward through the slender thermometer.

"Is it done yet?" Gigi asks, playing with Christopher on the kitchen floor. Joan has learned the best spot for the children to play while she is cooking is right in the heart of the kitchen with her.

"Not yet," Joan says, stooping over to make sure she is seeing the correct temperature. The temperature rises quickly during the first several minutes of cooking but seems to crawl for the last several, making Joan wonder if something is wrong with the thermometer. She stays stooped over, watching the red dye as it creeps toward 234 degrees. Before it reaches soft ball, she turns off the burner and removes the pan from the stove. Taking the thermometer out of the pot, she uses a spatula and adds the Marshmallow Fluff and peanut butter to the mixture, along with a teaspoon of vanilla. She stirs everything together and then pours the mixture into a buttered pan. "Who wants to lick the pan and the spoon?"

Gigi and Christopher are in front of her before she finishes the question, raising their little hands for the goodies. Joan leaves enough in the bowl for all three of them, and as the warm peanut butter fudge hits her tongue, she smiles in satisfaction. "Wow! So good."

"Yummy!" Gigi says, running her spoon around the bottom of the pan.

When the kids aren't looking, Joan uses her spoon and scoops some fudge from the pan. She remembers loving it this way as a child when her mom made it, warm and gooey right out of the pan. She looks at the soft brown fudge and hopes it will "set up," as her mom always said.

John lifts a long, thick slab of black walnut inside his workshop and sets it on the wood plane to begin the process of planing each side. He'll rotate the wood until it's approximately a one-and-a-quarter-inch square piece of lumber and thirty-one inches long and will repeat this for each leg before working on tapering them. He stops his work when Joan opens the door, letting the children run in ahead of her. She's holding a small plate in her hand. "Is that lunch?" he says, shutting off the planer.

"It's peanut butter fudge!" Gigi squeals. "It's yummy!" The little girl jumps up and down, waving her arms as if she's about to take flight.

"Is this Aunt DeeDee's peanut butter fudge?" John asks, taking the plate and lifting a piece. Joan nods. "There's nothing like it." He watches Gigi move busily around the workshop and smiles. "It looks like Mommy filled your tank with fudge because you have lots of energy!"

"Just eat some and you can do this, too," Gigi says, jumping.

He bites into a piece, closing his eyes. "Mmm. The best." He opens his eyes, looking at her as he pops the rest of the piece in his mouth. "Please tell me this means you'll be making it every year from now on."

"Yes, we will!" Gigi says, jumping higher yet into the air.

"I can't afford to make it every year," Joan says. "I think I've eaten half the pan by myself. I'll be enormous tomorrow."

John puts another piece of the fudge into his mouth. "It's worth being enormous one time a year for this." He hands the plate back to her. "What else are you making in there today?"

Joan bends down and picks up Christopher. "We like to surprise you when you come in for dinner. Don't we?" she says, looking at Gigi.

The little girl nods. "Yes! We like to surprise you with meat loaf!"

"That's not surprising Daddy," Joan says, laughing.

"It is surprising!" John says. "Mommy has never made meat loaf and I love it. Especially a meat loaf sandwich."

"What are you working on today?" Joan says, looking at the various pieces of wood in front of her.

"Legs!" John says, holding up a piece of the thick lumber. "If these can be half as good-looking as yours, I'll be happy."

Joan rolls her eyes. "Just what every woman wants . . . to have her legs compared to wood!"

"Wooden legs are beautiful!" John says. "They are stunning."

Joan reaches for Gigi's hand and walks to the door. "You're obsessed, John Creighton," she says, closing the door behind them.

"I'm not obsessed! I just know beauty when I see it, that's all." John looks at the piece of lumber in his hands. "Gorgeous!"

Miriam drives up to the door of Larry Maccabee's workshop and turns off the engine. "Andrea said that Larry had a couple of tables that might work for your house," she says, looking at Lauren.

"But what about the price? Larry's things are so expensive," Lauren says, getting out of the car and closing the door.

"The furniture *he* makes is expensive," Miriam says, opening the shop door. "If he refinishes something, it's usually less expensive. That's what we need to find!" She glances throughout the shop for Larry. "Larry! You've got customers!" Larry pops his head around the corner, wiping his hands on a rag. "You need a bell on your door."

"Who needs a bell when I've got a foghorn like you?" Lauren laughs out loud and Larry winks at her. "What can I help you ladies with?"

"When Andrea was here a couple of weeks ago," Miriam says, walking through the furniture pieces in the shop, "she said that you had some kitchen tables that look nice. Lauren is trying to find one for that dismal kitchen of hers."

Larry walks them toward a light-colored table with sleek, tapered legs. "I made this one out of tiger maple and finished it just a few—"

"Larry, you know as well as I do that Lauren and Travis cannot afford any tiger maple table that you made," Miriam says, cutting him off. "Show us the affordable ones."

"This really is beautiful, Larry," Lauren says, running her hand over the tabletop. "How long did—"

"He knows his work is beautiful," Miriam says. "He talks more about it than anybody else."

Larry shakes his head, laughing as he leads them toward another table. This one is round in a darker wood with simple legs. "This one is three hundred."

Miriam snarls her lip. "Three hundred for that? It's so small and plain."

"We don't have a big space," Lauren says. "And I think it's beautiful. I love how simple it is."

"I had to refinish it," Larry says. "At some point in time, someone went crazy with nail polish on the top of it. It was covered in dings as if somebody had taken a hammer or something to it. I think it was probably set up in a space for kids somewhere and got abused. I can't tell you how much I hate to see wood get abused."

"It looks brand-new," Lauren says.

Miriam sounds as if she is clearing rocks out of her throat. Lauren looks at her and Miriam bugs out her eyes. "It doesn't look new at all. This is clearly a used table that has almost been destroyed by wild children run amok with nail polish and hammers and whatnot."

"But the polish is all gone," Lauren says. "And it—"

"It has been used and abused," Miriam says, raising her voice over Lauren's. "Larry said so himself."

Larry laughs, shaking his head. "How about two seventy-five, Miriam?"

Lauren smiles. "That sounds won—"

"Two hundred," Miriam says, looking like she's chewing on lemons.

"Two seventy-five," Larry says.

"Two hundred," Miriam counters.

Larry looks at Lauren and she smiles, shrugging. "I think two seventy-five is fair," she says.

"Two hundred," Larry says, sticking his hand out in front of her.

"Really?!" Lauren says, laughing. "What just happened?"

"Skilled negotiations just happened," Miriam says, rapping her knuckles on the table.

SEVEN

May 2012

Travis is home from work when Lauren and Miriam arrive with the table in the back of Dalton's pickup truck. Travis refuses Miriam's or his pregnant wife's help in unloading the table. Setting the table down onto the driveway, he says, "This is awesome!"

"Do you really like it?" Lauren asks, rubbing her hand over the top of the table.

"I love it! It's the perfect size. Did Larry make it?"

Miriam scoffs. "If he had, no one in Grandon could have paid for it. Do you need help getting it inside?"

"I think I got it," Travis says, stretching his arms over the top and lifting it.

"Would you like me to take the card table that you've been using to the dump?" Miriam asks, following them into the house.

Lauren and Travis chuckle. "No, thanks!" Lauren says. "We will hold on to it and use it somewhere else."

"Where would you possibly use that thing? At an interrogation? All it needs is some torture tools lying on top of it and you're all set." Lauren giggles as Travis angles the table to get it through the kitchen doorway. Miriam watches as he maneuvers it and says, "We will tackle other parts of the house on another day."

Lauren hugs her good-bye. "I don't know what I would do without you and Gloria, Heddy, Stacy, Amy, Dalton, and . . ."

"Oh my! This is beginning to sound like all the 'begats' in the Bible," Miriam says, cutting her off. "Good-bye, my love!"

Lauren closes the front door and notices Travis bent over, looking beneath the table inside the kitchen. "It's cute, isn't it?"

He stands up straight, looking at her. "Yeah. You didn't tell me about this. That's a cool feature."

"What's a cool feature?" she says, walking into the kitchen.

"This little drawer underneath the table."

Lauren bends over to take a closer look. "I didn't even look underneath it at Larry's, and he loaded it for us so I never noticed. Does it open?"

Travis pulls open the drawer and they both look inside. To their surprise, they see something at the back of the drawer and pull it out farther to see what it is. Lauren reaches for several small stacks of what look to be index cards held tight with rubber bands. She removes a rubber band from one stack of cards and flips through them. "They're recipes." Travis looks over her shoulder. "Whoever sold the table to Larry must have forgotten that they were in there." She pulls her phone from her purse and dials Larry's number.

"Maybe someone wanted the recipes to go with the table," Travis says.

Lauren shakes her head. "I think someone forgot all about them. Look at these. They are all handwritten." She puts her hand in the air to indicate that Larry has picked up his phone. "Hi, Larry! It's Lauren. We just found a stack of recipes in the drawer of the table I bought. Do you remember who you bought it from? I'm sure they'll want them back."

"I don't remember. It's been too many years. I found the recipes when I started refinishing the table two weeks ago. I just kept them in there. I didn't feel right separating them from the table. Felt like they went together. They're yours now. Do you know how to cook?"

Lauren laughs. "Not exactly."

"Well, maybe these will get you on your way. You can do it," Larry says, sounding more like a father than just some guy who builds furniture in a too-dusty workshop on the other side of town.

"Thanks, Larry," Lauren says, hanging up. "He bought the table a few years ago and doesn't remember."

Travis looks at the recipes. "Here's one for meat loaf. I love meat loaf! Have you ever had a meat loaf sandwich?"

"No! Gross!"

Travis looks aghast. "You do *not* know what you're talking about! A meat loaf sandwich with mustard on it is transcendent."

Lauren grins, looking at him. "Do you even know what 'transcendent' means?"

"Yeah. It means meat loaf sandwich with mustard on it. Look it up." Lauren smiles as Travis flips through the recipes. "Here's one for peanut butter fudge. Peanut butter fudge! We could make meat loaf and peanut butter fudge tonight for dinner."

"Meat loaf and peanut butter fudge? For dinner?"

"There are worse things we could eat," Travis says, his face straight and serious.

She kisses his cheek. "I think tonight we will stick with hamburgers and try some of these other recipes later. Chicken enchiladas," she says, reading through some cards. "Strawberry cake. Red velvet cake. Homemade caramels. Muffins. Chicken casserole. Poppy seed dressing. Mmm." She lifts one of the cards, reading it: *"Val Clemente gave me this recipe for shortbread cookies ages ago. She said she thinks it came over on the Mayflower with her ancestors (not sure if that's true, but what a story!) and got passed down through the years. I always quadrupled the recipe because we ate these cookies like pigs! Enjoy!"* Lauren skims each one and looks down at the table, dreaming of mealtimes around it with her growing family.

Miriam leads Gloria, Andrea, Travis's cousin Gabe, and his wife, Amy, into Lauren's kitchen, setting an armload of drop cloths she was carrying onto the table. "All right!" Miriam says, clapping her hands together as if back at Glory's Place and getting the attention of the children. "First things first. We need to move the furniture into the center of each room and then put drop cloths on the floor."

"Miriam, we know how to paint," Gloria says, wearing a Grandon Tigers Baseball cap backward on her head. "We've had lots of experience with it over the years at Glory's Place."

"I am the supervisor, Gloria, and I am merely requesting excellence from all of you. I know that means that you will have to dig deep into your reservoir to find some sort of excellence, Gloria, but I simply must insist that you give us your best. Whatever that looks like coming from you."

Gloria looks at all the others around her. "Is it too late to appoint someone else as supervisor?"

The room erupts in laughter as Miriam waves her arms in the air. "Dalton, would you please cover that kitchen table? We can set the paint up there. Gabe and Travis? Would you bring in the paint and the ladders? Amy, if you could please do something with Gloria, taking her somewhere else in the house where I don't have to see that ridiculous hat, that would be wonderful."

"Me and my hat plan on working right next to you, Miriam," Gloria says, making Amy grin.

Dalton spreads a drop cloth over the table as Travis and Gabe set down the cans of paint. Gabe opens a can marked "Gray Harbor" and Gloria peers into it. "Is that green?"

"It's gray, Gloria," Miriam hisses.

Gloria shakes her head. "Well, it has green in it!"

Miriam points to the color of the paint. "It's called Gray Harbor, Gloria!"

"I think that says gray herb, because many herbs are green," Gloria says, winking at Gabe and Travis. "Where's the gray herb paint going?"

Miriam straightens her shoulders and takes a deep breath, but Lauren steps in next to her. "That one goes here in the kitchen, Gloria."

"Where you'll be using lots of herbs," Gloria says. "Smart choice!" She looks into the next can of paint. "Oh, blue!"

Miriam sighs loudly enough for the neighbors to hear. "It's gray, Gloria. Do you see the name? Gray Dawn."

Gloria bends closer as Travis stirs the paint. "It's a beautiful shade of blue. Where's this one going?"

"Our bedroom and the baby's room," Lauren says.

"Baby blue!" Gloria says. "I love it." She looks down at the third paint color that Gabe is opening. "Oh! Brown! Or do you call that taupe?"

Miriam shakes her head. "It's gray, Gloria! Gray Dream. Gray."

"I think I would have called it Brown Heaven."

Miriam purses her lips, staring at Gloria. "Brown Heaven?" Gloria nods. "That is so stupid! Who wants to go to a brown heaven?"

"Who wants a gray dream?" Gloria asks, opening her arms to everyone in the room. "No one here, Miriam. No one wants a gray dream. Only you. And frankly, I'm surprised your dreams have that much color."

Lauren picks up a paintbrush from the table and says,

"And this color goes in the living room and downstairs bathroom! So, who's painting which room?"

"I'm painting wherever Miriam is," Gloria says, raising a paintbrush high into the air.

"Then I will certainly be in some sort of brown heaven today," Miriam says.

"Amy and I can go upstairs," Gabe says, pouring some paint into smaller cans with grip handles for each of them.

"I'll take the bathrooms," Travis says.

"And I'll take the kitchen," Andrea says.

"With me," Lauren says, smiling.

"No ladders. No lifting. No moving things around," Travis says, instructing her.

"You're as bossy as Miriam," Lauren says, reaching for the container of paint he's poured for her.

"I heard that!" Miriam says from the living room, making Gloria cackle.

Andrea climbs onto the ladder in the kitchen and dips her paintbrush into the paint, placing it at an angle right next to the ceiling line of paint. Lauren watches her with interest. "Where'd you learn to do that?"

"We've moved five times in our marriage, and Bill and I have painted every room of each house! You just learn things."

"Did you know how to cook when you got married?"

Andrea smiles. "Like I said, you learn things. A good

recipe makes all the difference, I think. Do you like to cook?"

Lauren uses her paintbrush to cut in a straight line against the window. "Not really. I'm hoping to learn, though. We have to feed our kids more than hamburgers, right?"

"My kids would have loved hamburgers every night! Miriam says you bought a really cute table."

Lauren stops her work, looking up at her. "It probably sounds kind of stupid but I imagined me and Travis and our kids sitting around the table, eating together."

"That doesn't sound stupid," Andrea says, peering at Lauren over her shoulder.

"I don't remember doing that with my mom and dad, and I'd like to do it with my family." Lauren doesn't recall mealtimes with her own mom and dad. She has hazy memories of her dad before he went to prison, sitting on the sofa in their cramped apartment and eating a bowl of cereal now and then. Her mom never cooked, and when she began her jail stints, Lauren began the rounds of foster homes. She did have a couple of foster moms who were good cooks, especially Lori, from the last house she was in, but she remembers eating a lot of sandwiches and hot dogs growing up. To this day, if she never ate another hot dog again it would be fine with her.

"And you will enjoy lots of meals together around your table," Andrea says. "In a beautiful green kitchen."

"It's gray!" Miriam yells from the next room. "What is wrong with you people?"

Andrea and Lauren laugh out loud as Gloria hoots from the living room.

EIGHT

June 2012

When she finishes her shift in the floral department at Clauson's Supermarket, Lauren shops for ingredients she needs for some of the recipes she and Travis discovered inside the table drawer. "These are more groceries than you've ever bought," Ben says, bagging them. He drops one of the handwritten notes that has made him famous in Grandon into one of the sacks and places it inside her cart. "Are you having a party?"

"If I was," Lauren says, "you would be invited!" She leans closer to him, whispering. "I'm learning how to cook."

"Is someone teaching you?" Ben asks, his face lit up with the childlike wonder she loves most about him.

Lauren thinks for a moment. "Actually, yeah. Someone is teaching me." She gives him a quick hug before leaving. "Hopefully I'll be having you over real soon for dinner!"

She loads the groceries into her car, finds the sack that includes Ben's note, and reads it: *New things are ahead. Just be sure your eyes are open so you don't miss them! Have a great day, Ben.* She smiles, tucking the note inside the glove compartment, where she has kept every single note from Ben since she first met him.

She loves the way the kitchen now makes her feel with the fresh paint over the once-bland walls, and the cute table positioned right in front of the small bay window. The groceries are soon put away. Lauren pulls out the recipe for chicken enchiladas and sits down at the table, reading through the card once again.

Hello, my sweet girl! Your grandma and I worked together on these enchiladas and finally got the recipe to where it was a winner for all of you. Remember how many your dad ate each time I put these on the table?

Lauren looks at the handwriting with its perfect slant to the right and soft tails that trail the *m* and *n* and the curlicue atop the *o* and imagines a mother so unlike her own, a woman who obviously made dinner for her family each evening and then took the time to write down favorite recipes for her own child. She envisions them sitting down at the dinner table that now sits inside her own kitchen and wonders where they lived and in what era. She glances at the card.

These are nice and plump and perfect for company! The key

is making sure that the chicken is tender and not overbaked or overboiled. Follow these cooking instructions to a T and you'll have moist, tender chicken every time. And whatever you do, don't use milk, use whipping cream!

Lauren moves to the refrigerator and pulls out three chicken breasts, places them on a cutting board, and uses the bottom of her smallest pot to flatten them. She peeks at the recipe again:

Sprinkle each side with a little salt and pepper. Heat a skillet and when a sprinkle of water sizzles and hisses on top of it, add one tablespoon of butter. When the butter has melted, swirl it around in the skillet and place the chicken breasts into it. Cook for one minute only! Flip them over, turn down the heat to low, and put a lid on the skillet. Now this is important . . . do not lift that lid for ten minutes! When the ten minutes are up, you won't find any pink inside the chicken, but you will find a moist and tender breast. But only if you leave that lid in place for ten minutes! While the chicken is cooking, move on to making the sauce.

Lauren preheats the oven to 350°F and pulls the blender that she and Travis found at a garage sale to the front of the counter. She opens a four-ounce can of green chilies and dumps it into the blender, along with a fifteen-ounce can of diced tomatoes, an eighth of a cup of fresh cilantro leaves, an egg, three-quarters of a cup of whipping cream, and a dash of salt. She blends it together. With time remaining before she needs to check the chicken, she opens the packages of cheese and shreds two cups of the Monterey Jack and a half cup of the sharp cheddar. When the timer goes off on her phone, she lifts the lid of the skillet and stabs one of the chicken breasts with a fork, using a knife with the other hand to cut into it. "No pink," she says, impressed with herself. She places the chicken breasts onto a plate and lets them cool for a few minutes. When they are cool enough to touch, Lauren shreds each chicken breast with a fork and puts it into a bowl. She dices half an onion into small bits and scrapes it off of the cutting board and into the bowl, along with one cup of the Monterey Jack, and stirs it all together. Opening a package of small flour tortillas, she pulls one out and holds it in one hand while using the other to fill it with half a cup of the chicken mixture. She wraps the tortilla around the chicken mixture, and places it seam-side down in a nine-by-thirteen-inch pan, filling the pan with enchiladas and then pouring the sauce over all. She sprinkles a cup and a half of the Monterey Jack and cheddar cheese mixture over the top and places it inside the preheated oven. She reaches for the recipe.

I always serve these with sour cream, guacamole, Mexican rice, and salsa. I'm including the recipes for the Mexican rice, guacamole, and salsa, but you'll need to make the salsa way ahead of time. Remember how much time that always took? But remember how fresh it tasted and how much we'd laugh at Dad's impersonations? His Johnny Carson would leave us in tears! Now that you kids are grown, I haven't made this in ages. With just your dad and me here at home, meals are much smaller and quieter, but he still makes me laugh with his horrible impersonations. My sweet girl, I hope you have a noisy kitchen like I did! I loved those days. They went so fast. Enjoy these with your family!

Lauren feels a pang of sadness as she reads the words and can't imagine how the owner of these cards feels, no longer having these recipes. She reasons that maybe these cards are much older than she thinks and perhaps "sweet girl" has passed away. While the enchiladas bake, she moves on to making the Mexican rice and guacamole. Homemade salsa will have to wait until another day, along with any impersonations that Travis might try.

July 1972

Joan walks to the front desk at the doctor's office, holding Christopher in her arms. Gigi stayed with John to "help Daddy with the table." Joan can only imagine how happy John will be to see her pull into the driveway after her appointment. The doctor's office called her this morning, leaving a message with John, saying she needed to return to the office. She had her yearly checkup just last week and realized she had not given the office their newest insurance information. "I'm Joan Creighton," she says to the receptionist. "I was here last week but forgot to give you my new insurance information. Someone called my husband this morning."

"Mrs. Creighton," the receptionist says, holding a finger in the air. "One moment."

Joan is surprised to see Dr. Burns walk to the front of the office; she normally stays busy going from one room to the next, visiting with her patients. Dr. Burns has delivered both of her children and has short dark hair peppered with gray and has always had a kind, gentle way about her. "Hi, Joan," Dr. Burns says, squeezing Christopher's chubby thigh. "Come on back." She leads Joan into her office, a small space filled with pictures of Dr. Burns's family and pictures drawn by her grand-daughter.

"I forgot to leave my new insurance information," Joan says.

Dr. Burns indicates the sofa and Joan sits down, holding Christopher on her lap. Dr. Burns walks to her desk, lifts a manila file folder off it, and sits next to Joan on the couch. "I'm sorry there was confusion with the phone call this morning, Joan. This isn't about insurance. We got the results back from your mammogram. You have breast cancer."

Christopher turns to pat Joan's face and she realizes she isn't breathing. "What does that mean . . . exactly?"

"It means we're going to get you in to see the best cancer doctor in the area. I've already called Dr. Kim and have made an appointment for you to see her on Friday. Is that okay?"

Joan is still processing the words. "Yes. Of course." Her eyes are full when she looks at Dr. Burns. "I'm awfully young for breast cancer, right?"

"Cancer has no respect for any of us," she says. She squeezes Christopher's foot. "But this little guy makes you brave." Joan pulls the baby to her and kisses his head. "I'm here anytime you need me, Joan."

After setting Christopher on his little car seat and buckling it, she sits next to him in the backseat of the car and feels the tears forming. He pounds on the padding in front of him and Joan wipes her eyes before the tears fall. "That's right!" she says, smacking the padding. "Let's go home!" She kisses his hand and exhales loudly. It's time to make dinner for her family.

NINE

July 1972

John pulls into the garage and turns off the car before jumping out and running around to the passenger side, where he helps Joan out, wrapping his arm around her waist. Dr. Kim wasted no time in beginning chemotherapy, explaining that she wanted to reduce the tumor inside of Joan's breast before performing surgery. This is Joan's third week in a row, and each time she's left nauseous and depleted of energy the day following treatment, but on this Saturday, she woke up feeling more energy than usual, and while her mom took care of Gigi and Christopher for a couple of hours, Joan thought that she and John could enjoy lunch at their favorite restaurant. Their time together was cut short; Joan got sick halfway through, too nauseous to eat. She holds on to John as he leads her up the garage stairs and into the house, where he helps her to their bedroom and into the bed. He unties her sneakers and slips them off her feet. She lies back on her pillow and covers her face with her hand, moving it through her hair. Wisps, fine and long, entwine between her fingers, and she holds her hand in front of her. John removes the hair, setting it on the nightstand for now, and clasps his hand in Joan's. Her eyes fill with tears as she reaches for her hair again with the other hand. John stops her hand and holds on to that one as well. A tear sneaks down her cheek and he kisses one of her hands. "It doesn't matter. It'll grow back."

"I'm going bald," she says, her voice squeaking.

"Big deal. My dad's bald. You don't see him crying about it." She laughs out loud and more tears fall over her cheeks. He wipes them away with his hand and smiles at her. "You could be bald and wear a burlap sack and still be beautiful."

She shakes her head. "I don't want the kids to watch me go bald."

His eyes brighten. "Then have them do it for you." She looks up at him as he nods. "Today. They've seen you buzz my hair. They can use the clippers and do it for you."

"Gigi would love that," Joan says, squeezing his hand.

"And she can tie her favorite scarf around your head."

Joan begins to laugh. "She'll pick that awful bandanna we use to play pirates."

64

"And you will be the prettiest pirate I've ever seen." Another tear makes its way down Joan's cheek and John wipes it away.

July 2012

Gloria walks into her office and discovers a cheeseball surrounded by gingersnap cookies on her desk. A typewritten note on top says: *A chocolate chip cheeseball for the hardworking staff and volunteers at Glory's Place.* "Too bad Miriam can't have some," Gloria says beneath her breath as she uses the plastic knife left with the cheeseball to put some on a gingersnap and takes a bite. "Mmm! Oh my!" Andrea and Amy hear her as they pass and stick their heads in her door. "Mmm!" Gloria says, raising the plate into the air. "Come try this. Someone left these for us."

"Who left them?" Amy asks, taking a bite of a cookie.

"The note doesn't say," Gloria answers, shoving the rest of the cookie in her mouth. "Has to be Betty trying something new for her catering side."

"Then why didn't she put this in a Betty's Bakery box?" Amy asks, making yummy noises in the back of her throat.

Andrea puts some on a cookie and takes a bite, her eyes widening. "This is yummy!"

"My mother used to make cheeseballs," Gloria says, reaching for another cookie. "But not like this one."

Dalton and Miriam peek inside the office to check on the afternoon schedule and to see which station they'll be manning first. "Dalton!" Gloria yells. "Come get a cookie with this on it." He and Miriam step toward her and Gloria holds her hand in the air, stopping Miriam. "No Miriam. I've seen you eat cookies. Stay back."

Miriam scowls at her as Andrea laughs. "Be nice, Gloria. She doesn't eat that many."

Gloria snaps her head to look at Andrea. "How do you think Cookie Monster got his name?" She points at Miriam. "Right here."

"You are so rude, Gloria," Miriam says, snatching a cookie from the plate and putting some of the cheeseball on top, making sure she gets plenty of chocolate chips.

When Lauren enters the front door, Gloria waves at her through the office window. "A sweet for the sweet," she says, holding up the plate. "And to answer the question you're about to ask, no, we don't know where this came from, but I'm thinking Betty's Bakery."

"Mmm. Delicious," Lauren says.

"Tell us! Tell us!" Gloria says, taking another bite. "How'd the appointment go?"

Lauren grins, chewing the cookie. "Dr. Flores says that Christmas will be extra special this year."

Gloria claps her hands together. "A Christmas baby!"

"December eighteenth," Lauren says. "Just a few days before our anniversary, but after the annual fund-raiser."

"You'll have a solid week of one celebration after another," Miriam says, sounding as if she's delivering a death notice. "It will be like delivering a baby in the Arctic." She shivers at the thought.

"Women have babies in the Arctic, Miriam," Gloria says. "You know what? You complain too much! You complained last year when they decided to have an outside wedding in December. You survived."

Miriam is aghast. "I was a Popsicle at the end of that ceremony!"

Gloria shakes her head. "No, you weren't. Popsicles are sweet."

Miriam ignores her as both of her hands fly to her head. "We have so much left to do to get your home ready for the baby!"

"The baby could come today and would have a beautiful, safe, and loving home to live in," Gloria says.

"Safe and loving it is," Miriam says, refusing to call the home beautiful. "We'll add a few more touches to it and it will be ready for the baby!"

The thought gives Lauren butterflies in her stomach. In less than five months she and Travis will be parents.

July 1972

Joan sits on a chair in the middle of the kitchen with Christopher on her lap and a towel draped around her shoulders. John holds the hair clippers between his hands as if he's about to make a presentation of them to royalty. "Hear ye! Hear ye! By order of the palace, Queen Joan shall be shorn on this day of her golden locks."

"What does that mean?" Gigi asks, reaching up so she can hold the clippers.

"It means," John says, still using an affected royal voice. "That Princess Gigi and Prince Christopher shall buzz off their mother's hair." He bows to Gigi. "I shall plug them in and thou shalt begin said buzzing."

"Really, Mommy?" Gigi asks, resting her hands on top of Joan's knees.

Joan nods. "Yep! Buzz away!"

"But you'll be all bald like Grandpa!" Gigi says.

"I know," Joan says, laughing. "But my hair will grow back." She leans in, whispering. "No such luck for Grandpa!"

"Princess!" John says, bowing low again and presenting the clippers. Gigi takes them and John plugs the cord into a wall outlet. He shows her where to turn them on, and she giggles as she brings them up to her mother's head. John helps her move them from the front of Joan's head to the back, and her long, brown strands collect on top of her shoulders or fall to the floor like strands of silk. He notices Joan's face; her eyes are filled with tears, and he reaches out for her hand, smiling. Christopher wriggles on Joan's lap, wanting to help his sister, and John takes him in his arms, holding him so he can use the clippers, too. Gigi takes a few more strokes with the clippers and then deems that the work is finished. John sets Christopher back on Joan's lap and reaches for the clippers from Gigi. "Thank you, Princess Gigi and Prince Christopher! Now, in order for the queen not to look like a crazy person, I shall buzz off these straggling tufts of hair that make her look like a baby bird." Joan laughs out loud and Gigi squeals at the sight of her mom. "Perhaps the princess has a lovely scarf for the queen to wear upon her cranium." Gigi screws up her face, looking at him. He leans down to her and speaks in his regular voice. "Do you have a scarf that Mommy can wear on her head?"

"Yes!" Gigi shouts, running from the kitchen. She returns moments later, waving a red-and-black bandanna in the air. "I got it!" Joan looks over her shoulder and cackles at the sight of the bandanna they use to play pirates with, shaking her head.

"Thank you, Princess Gigi," John says, continuing in his royal herald voice. He ties the bandanna around Joan's head and bows down in front of her, lifting her hand. "I would like to present to the royal court, the Queen Pirate Mother of this palace . . . the only one able to have someone beheaded and steal booty from seagoing vessels." Joan laughs, watching him. "The only one powerful enough to subdue other kingdoms and get into a swashbuckling sword fight atop a pirate ship. Please rise for the royal Queen Pirate Mother, Joan Creighton." Gigi and Christopher clap as Joan stands. John wraps his arm around her and kisses her face. "The most beautiful Queen Pirate Mother in all the land," he says in his own voice, making her smile.

TEN

July 2012

Lauren flips through the recipes from inside the table drawer and finds the one she was looking for: German Apple Pancake. She had read through the recipe a few days earlier and realized that with the time it took to mix together and bake, she would need to make it on a Saturday morning. She hears the mower outside the kitchen window and knows that Travis will be out there for at least an hour finishing the mowing and weed eating around their home. She sits down at the table, holding her cup of coffee as she reads the recipe.

Do you remember how many times the kids at school told you that they did not eat breakfast and when you would tell them about what you had eaten even that morning, they were always shocked! How our family loved breakfast! It was so hectic inside our small kitchen on those school mornings, but sitting here today, I sure do

71

miss the noise. Every time I made this we would scrape every last bite from the skillet. Somehow, time kept fast-forwarding and this became too big for me and Dad. He always loved it with bacon and the rest of us preferred sausage. It's yummy with both. Granny Smith apples are tasty in this, but so are Macintosh. You'll need to cook the Granny Smith for a few minutes in the skillet before popping it into the oven because they take longer to get tender than Macintosh. I hope you enjoy it as much as we did when you were growing up and that your family scrapes every last bite from the skillet, too!

As she stands up to prepare the ingredients, Lauren tries to imagine again how many children grew up in this house and what mealtimes must have looked like for their family. She peels three Granny Smith apples, cuts the core from each, and then cuts them into thin slices before making the batter of eggs, flour, whipping cream, butter, salt, nutmeg, and vanilla. She prepares a mixture of white sugar, cinnamon, and nutmeg and sets it beside the stove. When a quarter cup of butter has melted inside the skillet, she sprinkles half of the sugar mixture over it and then places the apple slices on top. As the recipe instructs, she puts a lid on the skillet for three to four minutes as the apples get a little tender. The smell of the apples fills the kitchen with an aroma that reminds Lauren of Betty's Bakery. "Watch out, Betty! I'm coming for ya!" she says, smiling. She sprinkles the remaining sugar mixture over the apples and then pours the batter on top, waiting until it bubbles before removing the skillet from the stove and setting it inside the oven. She turns on the oven light and looks inside. Without any experience, she never thought she would be able to follow a recipe, but each of these recipe cards is written in such a way that's easy to understand. The simple language makes the food sound delicious, enticing Lauren to try each dish. In a way that she can't explain, she hopes that this mother would be proud of her.

Bacon is sizzling when Travis opens the garage door that leads into the kitchen. "Is that bacon I smell?" he says, grinning. He notices the apple pancake sitting on top of the stove. "Holy mackerel! What is that?"

Lauren giggles as he marches to the stove and leans down to take a whiff. "It's a German Apple Pancake."

He stares at her and back at the apple pancake. "Who are you and what have you done with my wife? I was coming in for a bowl of cereal."

She laughs at him, swatting his hand away before he can touch the pan. "Go wash your hands! The bacon will be ready when you get back." Travis was right; if they ate breakfast, it was normally a bowl of cereal, but she has a feeling all of that is going to change. She sets the bacon on a plate covered with a paper towel, slices the apple pancake, and calls Travis to breakfast.

August 1972

Joan pulls on a pair of drawstring pants and cinches them tight around her waist. Her already petite frame has lost enough weight that the jeans and slacks she was wearing just two months ago no longer fit. She still tries out her mom's recipes, but the smell of the food ultimately makes her nauseous and she ends up nibbling at the food, at best. Her mom and mother-in-law have taken turns making meals and freezing them for ease, but when she's able, Joan wants to be in the kitchen with Gigi and Christopher.

"Are you feeling good, Mommy?" Gigi asks, peeking her head inside her mom and dad's bedroom.

Joan hates that cancer has made her five-year-old tiptoe around her at times, wondering if she's too sick to play a game, take her to the park, or cook together in the kitchen. "I'm feeling awesome!" she says, fibbing.

"Then what's for breakfast?" Gigi asks, leaning against the bed.

"How about scones or Grandma's cinnamon loaf? Of course, that needs to rise, so it will take a long time, but just think of that warm, buttery, cinnamony goodness with pecans on top!"

Gigi thinks for a second. "What's the shorter thing you said?"

"Scones." Joan tidies her bed as she talks. Even on her worst days she likes to make the bed, convinced that it helps her feel better. "It's like a yummy, heavy biscuit with blueberries, raspberries, chocolate chips, cinnamon, or whatever we want to put inside them. Grandma used to make them for me when I was your age."

"Mmm!" Gigi says, helping her mom make the bed. "Chocolate chips, please!"

Joan laughs. "I knew you would say that. Did Daddy already leave for work?"

Gigi nods, tossing a throw pillow onto the bed. "I think so. I couldn't find him when I came downstairs."

John has been going to work earlier each day with the heating and air-conditioning repair company so he can be home by midafternoon when Joan's energy falls out beneath her. John lives out the "sickness and health" part of his vows in a way that brings daily tears to Joan's eyes.

"You didn't sign up for this," she told him after she couldn't make it to the bathroom after her second round of chemo and vomited on their bedroom floor.

"Yes, I did," he told her matter-of-factly. "So did you. I might cash in your vow someday, so take notes."

She wanted to laugh, but another wave of nausea made her double over. John grabbed her and carried her into the bathroom, where she vomited into the toilet. "What about your table, John?" she said after the last wave was finished.

"That's what you're thinking as you stare into the toilet?" She nodded her head. "A toilet makes you think of the table I'm building?" She began to snicker. "Really? A toilet? How offensive is that?"

She laughed out loud, clutching her stomach. "Don't make me laugh, John!"

"Then don't compare my table to a toilet."

Her voice echoed off the bathroom walls as she howled, reaching for his hand. He helped her to her feet and flushed the toilet, easing her to the sink. "I'm not comparing the table to a toilet," she said, rinsing her face and brushing her teeth as she giggled. She turned to look at him and he handed her a towel. "You wanted it finished by October and that's when you were able to work on it after work and an hour or two on the weekend. Now all of your time after work is taken up in here."

He helped her back into bed. "My time isn't 'taken up,' Joan. My time is used exactly the way I want to use it." He pulled the blankets over her thin frame and leaned down to kiss her. "So, I'll have it done by Thanksgiving instead of October. No big deal." He thought for a moment. "Maybe the extra time will help me figure out how to make it less like a toilet."

"Daddy has gotten so good at sneaking out of the house each morning that none of us hears him," Joan says, smiling at Gigi.

"He's like a cat!"

"He is like a cat," Joan says. "Your brother still sleeping?"

"I think so. I haven't heard him singing yet." They always knew when Christopher was awake because his tiny voice could be heard trying to sing the songs Joan sang to him, using whatever words he could say, but most of it was babble that made Joan, John, and Gigi laugh while outside the door, listening.

"All right," Joan says, leading the way into the kitchen. "Let's find Grandma's scone recipe and get to work!"

ELEVEN

August 2012

Lauren and Andrea lead the children outside at Glory's Place and watch as they scatter across the playground. Andrea notices as Lauren puts her hand on her small baby bump. "Are you still bothered with morning sickness?"

Lauren nods. "Just when I think it's gone it sweeps over me again. Did you have it?"

"For my second child," Andrea says. "My first pregnancy was a breeze, so I thought my next pregnancy would be the same. I actually lost weight the first four months when I carried my second."

They sit on a bench next to the swings, where they can see all of the children. "Were you afraid for your first one?" Lauren asks, tying five-year-old Aaron's shoe when he thrusts it in front of her.

Andrea chuckles. "I was afraid for both of them! For each pregnancy, Bill and I always said, 'I hope we don't mess this one up!'"

"How did you know what to do?" Lauren asks, shielding her eyes from the sun so she can get a better view of the children on the slide. "One at a time," she yells.

"Well, you figure it out together. It's funny because you get a marriage license, a driver's license, a fishing license, business license, or whatever, but there is no parent license. You just have a baby and you're a parent! No paperwork and no classes required. Bill and I were a team and we trusted each other. You and Travis are a great team! I don't think you have anything to worry about."

"I feel like there are lots of things to worry about!" Lauren says, chuckling. "There's a lot to know."

"Yeah, but you learn it," Andrea says, brushing mulch and dirt off of Molly's legs after she falls in front of them.

"The world seems kind of crazy now."

Andrea nods. "We thought the same thing when we started having kids. Bill and I learned that's there's only so much we could do as parents. We did everything we could to teach and guide our kids, but we learned that there are things that only God can do. We learned to pray when we became parents," she says, laughing. "One thing we did was we asked other parents who had older kids what they did, and we used the advice that worked best for us.

Some of the most common advice was to get our baby on a schedule and to keep that schedule. As each child grew, we put them on a schedule that was appropriate for their age."

Lauren thinks for a moment. "I don't think my mom ever had me . . . or herself . . . on a schedule. When I went into my first foster home, I couldn't believe they said my bedtime was nine o'clock! I always stayed up until eleven or midnight." Her face clouds over as she looks across the playground. "What if I'm like my mom?"

"You're not," Andrea says.

Lauren turns her head to look at her. "How do you know?"

"Because you just asked that question."

Lauren pulls out the recipe for creamy spinach soup from among the cards in the table drawer and begins to read through it again.

Someone once told me by the time a child is five their eating habits are already established. I started you kids on vegetables and healthy food when you were just toddling around here and you're still healthy eaters today! The green of this soup was never an issue because you loved the taste. Remember when Dad got so sick that one winter? I was practically spoon-feeding this along with tomato soup and chicken soup to him, and he got better quicker than the doctor expected! I always got our milk and cream from Bud's. Remember going with me to the farm? I'm convinced the cows on his farm produced the best milk around, and it was worth the drive there every week. Use good half-and-half, fresh spinach, and farm-fresh chicken for this, and your kids will love it as much as you did.

Lauren pounds out a couple of boneless chicken breasts and puts them into a skillet to cook and glances again at the recipe. *Dice half a cup of onion and half a cup of red pepper. Make sure you make the dices small. They should blend into the soup, not stick out.* Lauren is careful as she dices, paying attention that the onion and red pepper are as small as she can make them, before placing them in a pot with a tablespoon of melted butter. She sautés them for a few minutes before adding one pound of thawed, chopped spinach, two cups of chicken stock, and two crushed garlic cloves. She looks at the recipe card again and moans: *Salt and pepper to taste, and a touch of cayenne pepper. Just figure out what your family likes and season the soup according to that.* "What does that even mean?" Lauren says aloud, sprinkling a bit of salt into the soup.

As it cooks for ten minutes, she melts a quarter cup of butter in a saucepan, adds a quarter cup of flour to it, and begins whisking it over low heat. *Don't let it scorch! Whisk for two minutes,* the recipe says. After measuring out three cups of half-and-half, she pours it into the flour mixture and whisks until it is blended. Then she pours it into the pot with the spinach, letting it simmer for ten minutes. She wonders how much of a difference this half-and-half and chicken is that she purchased at Clauson's, compared to what she could buy on a farm somewhere. She's not familiar with any local farms, let alone one called Bud's, and assumes the table she purchased and these recipes came from another town, or even another state. She hasn't lifted the lid of the skillet since she began cooking the chicken, and when the ten minutes are up, she checks on it, and it is perfect. She cuts the breasts into small pieces and adds it to the soup, turns the stove burner off and covers the soup. *To let the flavors blend,* as the recipe card says.

One day, she hopes to venture out and make the crusty bread that went along with this recipe, but for tonight she'll make grilled cheese sandwiches. She lifts the lid of the soup, spoons out a yummy-looking bite, and lets it cool before tasting it. Just as the recipe card instructed, she seasons it with a bit more salt, pepper, and cayenne pepper, and tastes it again. "So good," she says to herself, looking into the pot. Andrea was right: she's nothing like her mom.

TWELVE

September 1972

John makes his way to the workshop after Joan and the children are in bed. He hasn't had the chance to be out here in over two weeks and picks up the table leg he started working on over a month ago. Standing it on top of the worktable, he tries to size it up, thinking about his next step, but he can't think and pushes his forehead against the leg, tears pooling in his eyes. He shuts his eyes tight against them. He drove Joan to a follow-up appointment with Dr. Kim today and expected to take her out for lunch at her favorite restaurant.

"The cancer has spread to your lungs," Dr. Kim said. "We need to be more aggressive with your treatment."

Joan's eyes filled with fear as John said, "Can you stop it? Can it go anywhere else?"

"We will try everything we can to stop it," Dr. Kim

said. "Yes, it could continue to spread. I've consulted with Dr. Levy, who is the best surgeon for this type of cancer, and my office will set up an appointment for you to meet with him as soon as possible."

"I'll need surgery?" Joan asked.

"*If* you need surgery," Dr. Kim said, "Dr. Levy is the most qualified. We won't know anything until he runs more tests." She stepped away from her desk and sat next to Joan on the sofa in her office. "We'll do everything we can, Joan, but you need to fight this. You need to stay positive and strong. Can you do that?" Tears covered Joan's eyes, but she nodded. "I don't know everything about this disease, Joan, but I promise you that I'll fight alongside you." Dr. Kim squeezed Joan's hand and a tear fell over Joan's cheek.

John did not ask about prognosis; he couldn't bear to hear it, but deep down he knew. He could sense it in Dr. Kim's voice and see it in her eyes. They set up the appointment to see Dr. Levy early the next week, and he took hold of Joan's hand, leading her out of the office, through the parking lot, and to the car. He noticed again how fragile her hand had become just in the last month. As each day passed, he was convincing himself that she was getting better, but all that had changed today.

"John." Joan's voice was small. "What if—"

"No!" he said. "There is no 'what if,' Joan."

She turned to look at him in the car. "Yes, there is. We both know there is."

"We will do other things in addition to surgery and medication and treatments and whatever," he said, grabbing her hand.

"What other things?"

He looked out the front window, staring at the Chevy pickup truck in the parking lot. "I don't know. We'll pray."

"We are not praying people, John."

"Then we will become praying people!" John snapped, controlling his voice. "We will find people who pray."

She smiled. "John, you and I both know many people who have been prayed for and they died anyway."

He nodded. "And lots have been prayed for and they're still living today. Shouldn't we at least try?"

John sets the table leg back down and puts his hands on the worktable, leaning on it. Tears drip onto the table, turning brown sawdust into a rich coffee color. "I don't pray," he says aloud. "I don't know how. But I believe in you, God. I always have, I think. Ever since my grandparents told me about you when I was little. Even though my family never went to church, even though Joan and I don't go, I believe you are who you say you are. I believe that you made the world. I believe that you're the one who raised Jesus out of that grave. And I believe that you can heal Joan." He begins to sob as he leans onto the work-table. "I know you can. Will you? Please. Please, God. Will you do something for her that only you can do?" His throat fills and he can't finish.

September 2012

Gloria enters her office and smiles; a paper plate covered with pieces of cake sits on top of her desk. It looks like a small breakfast cake, filled with blueberries. She takes a bite and closes her eyes. "Mmm," she says, smacking the desk.

"What's wrong with you?" Miriam says, sticking her head in the office door. Gloria has taken another bite but points to the cake. "The food bandit strikes again!" Miriam says, reaching for a piece.

"'Bandit' is a horrible word," Gloria says with her mouth full. "A bandit takes things. This is more like a food Santa!"

Miriam bites into the cake and smacks the desk as well. "Do we know who our secret Santa is yet?"

Gloria shakes her head, finishing the last bite in her hand. "No! I wonder if it's one of those things like you see in movies—where once you find out who's doing it, everything stops from that point on."

Miriam stares at her. "What movie has ever had that story line?"

"The one that I just told you about!"

Miriam sighs, shaking her head. "And we're sure Betty isn't dropping these things off? Like maybe she's trying out new recipes for the bakery?"

"She swore to me it's not her," Gloria says, reaching for another piece of cake.

"Well, whoever it is, they need to open a bakery!" Miriam says.

"Miriam!" Gloria mumbles with her mouth full. "What if Betty hears?"

"I didn't mean here in Grandon," Miriam says, whispering. "I meant in the next town, which is far enough away from Betty's, but also close enough for me to drive to."

Gloria nods. "Candy, muffins, cupcakes, orange cake . . ."

"And it had just a hint of orange! It wasn't overpowering, but so delicious!" Miriam says, remembering the moist cake left a few days earlier. She makes a satisfied noise in her mouth as she holds up a piece of breakfast cake. "These blueberries are fresh. And there's a hint of lemon. Do you taste it?"

"Do I taste it?" Gloria says. "Do you think I'm hard of tasting? Of course I taste it!"

As Dalton and Heddy, Amy, Stacy, and Lauren come in for the day, Gloria waves each of them into her office for a piece of cake. "How are we ever going to thank the person doing this?" Dalton says.

"We can't thank them," Gloria says. "That would ruin everything."

"How?" Heddy asks.

"Well, it would be just like that movie that Gloria saw," Miriam says, rolling her eyes. "You know, the one about where food was being secretly delivered, but once the person was discovered, then the deliveries stopped."

"Aha!" Gloria says, pointing at her. "You have seen that movie!"

"There is no such movie!" Miriam says, leaving the office.

Gloria runs to her office door and leans out into the entryway. "You just described the plot, so I know you've seen it, Miriam!" She turns around and puts her finger to her lips. "Shh. We don't want to spoil this." She puts the rest of the cake she was eating into her mouth. "Let's just keep our mouths closed so this doesn't stop and simply say, 'God bless our secret Santa.'"

THIRTEEN

September 1972

"What are you doing?" John asks, entering the kitchen.

"I'm going to make pumpkin ricotta pancakes with Gigi," Joan says, pulling butter, eggs, ricotta cheese, and milk from the refrigerator.

John stands in front of the sink, looking at her. "You have surgery today. You can't eat."

"But you can eat. And Gigi and Christopher can eat."

"You don't have to do this, Joan."

"I knew you would say that," she says, pulling a mixing bowl from a cupboard. "I know what I do and don't have to do, John." Her voice is cracking and he's sorry he said anything. "Gigi is old enough that she will have memories. I remember my mom in the kitchen. I can still smell some of the things she made for us when I was growing up. I don't want Gigi to remember me or you looking scared on the day that I went to the hospital. I want her to remember her mom in the kitchen, making her breakfast." Her voice cracks and John steps to her, wrapping his arms around her.

"I think she needs to remember her mom *and* dad in the kitchen making breakfast for her!" He yells over the top of Joan's head, "Hey, Gigi!" They hear her small voice answering from her bedroom at the top of the stairs. "Come on down! We're making pancakes for breakfast!" They can hear her feet slap onto the floor and then break out into a run for the stairs.

"You're helping, too, Daddy," she says, coming down the stairs and turning the corner into the kitchen.

"I'm helping, too, and no matter what Mommy says, I'm loading the pancakes with chocolate chips!"

Joan laughs and breaks two eggs into the mixing bowl. "If you're both helping, then you both need to wash your hands."

John opens a pack of ground sausage he recently bought at the butcher and begins to form patties as Gigi helps Joan pour in the rest of the ingredients to make the batter. "Remember," John says to Gigi, "it's all in the stirring. If you don't use your magic wand then the pancakes are ruined." Gigi looks at Joan and Joan hands her a whisk. Gigi attempts to put it into the bowl when John stops her. "Nuh-uh! You can't put that in there without waving it over the bowl and saying the magic words."

"What magic words?" Gigi says.

"Eatem, eatem! Eatem uppem!"

Joan smiles and Gigi giggles, waving the whisk over the bowl. "Eatem, eatem! Eatem uppem!" she says, thrusting the whisk into the mixture and stirring it as if her life depends on it.

"How many pancakes will you eat?" Gigi asks her dad.

John lifts up his shirt, sticking out his belly so it's round and firm, like a bowling bowl. He slaps it like a drum and snarls his upper lip, using a funny voice. "I'm thinking eighty is a good number."

Gigi and Joan both laugh and he keeps his stomach sticking out as they finish cooking. They work together inside the small kitchen and Joan finds herself smiling throughout. If she wanted Gigi to have a memory, then John was going to do whatever he could to make it a lasting one. When the pancakes, sausages, strawberries, and blueberries are on the table and Christopher is in his high chair, Gigi spreads her arms open and says, "Welcome to our feast!"

"It is a feast!" John says. "And I'm extremely grateful for your mommy, who cooked it." He looks at Joan and her mouth turns up into a sad smile.

"Are you done talking, Daddy?" Gigi asks.

John laughs and rubs his eyes with the palms of his hands. "I am, sweetie. Go ahead and eat."

They would explain again to Gigi that Joan would be going in for surgery today and would be gone for a few days, but for now they ate, and they laughed together, just as Joan had hoped.

July 2012

Lauren pulls a gallon of whole milk from the fridge and sets it on the counter. She picks up the recipe card for *Homemade Yogurt* and reads through it again.

I wonder how many gallons of homemade yogurt I made as you were growing up. Once I made that first batch, there was no turning back! Your dad said, "I will never be able to eat store-bought yogurt again." And as far as I know, he hasn't! For a slightly sweet yogurt, include less than one-third cup of sugar, but if you like it unsweet, don't add the sugar. Either way it is delicious and, like you always said, "Filled with strength and nutrients!" We'd dollop this on waffles and always ate in on the side with pancakes or oatmeal casserole, and we made countless yogurt parfaits! Again, I only used milk from Bud's farm, but if you move away, I hope you can find fresh milk at a local farm near you. Remember, don't let the milk get over 200°F while it is on the stove, and when it cools, don't let it go below 100°F.

Lauren flips the card over and reads the directions:

Pour one gallon of milk into a pot and heat it to 180°F to 200°F. Scrape off the skin from the top and let it cool to between 100°F and 110°F. Add one cup of whole yogurt as a starter, one to two tablespoons of vanilla, and not quite one-third cup of sugar (or no sugar at all). Stir it all together, put a lid on it, and place it inside the oven with the oven light on. If your oven has two oven lights, it will get too warm. If you do have two lights, just let the oven heat up for an hour or so and then turn the oven lights off. If you only have one oven light, you can keep it on for the next eight to twelve hours. (Some people put the pot on a heating pad to keep warm, but I think the oven works better. To each his own.) Take the pot out of the oven and line a large colander with food-grade cheesecloth. Put the colander inside a large bowl and pour the yogurt into it. Set it inside the fridge to let it drain to the consistency you love! I have forgotten to put the colander inside a bowl and trust me, you end up with a mess! Give it a stir and put it into a container. Will keep for up to two weeks and boy, oh boy, is it ever yummy! Don't let the idea of homemade yogurt scare you. You watched me make it countless times. Now try it yourself. She included four happy faces that each had hair of different lengths and some faces wore glasses. Lauren looks at each face, wondering if they represent individual family members.

Lauren lets the milk cool to 110°F as she gets ready for Glory's Place and then adds the cup of yogurt, tablespoon of vanilla, and about a quarter cup of sugar. She covers it with a lid and places it inside the oven and turns the oven light on. "Hmm," she says. "I can't imagine this is going to work."

When she arrives at Glory's Place, she sticks her head inside Gloria's office. "Hi, Gloria! Any more goodies today?"

Gloria shakes her head. "I wish. How are you feeling, babe?"

"Pretty good! It feels like my baby bump is getting bigger."

Gloria stands up from her desk to take a better look. "I don't see a bump. If you want to see a bump, take a look at Miriam's."

"I heard that, Gloria!" Miriam says from the entryway.

Lauren turns as if headed to the big room, but stops, looking back at Gloria. "Hey, Gloria! Have you ever heard of a farmer named Bud in this area?"

Gloria's mouth turns down as she thinks. "That name doesn't ring a bell. What kind of farmer?"

"I think a dairy farmer."

"Dairy farmer. No, I don't know of one, but I haven't been here as long as others. Check with Dalton or Heddy. Why are you trying to find him?"

Lauren shrugs. "I just heard that he had a dairy farm. Was wondering about buying some fresh milk."

"Ah, looking into healthier foods for you and the baby!

I know that Neil Wassman sells milk out on Portland Road, if that helps."

"Thanks, Gloria!" Lauren makes her way to the lockers and wonders if Neil Wassman knows of Bud, or if Bud is even from Grandon or the area. If she could track down Bud, maybe she could track down the owner of the recipe cards and give them back to her. She knows it's a long shot, but if they were her cards, filled with so many family memories, she would want them back. The least she can do is try to find him.

FOURTEEN

September 1972

John puts money into the vending machine and watches as a paper cup drops into place. He pushes the button for coffee, and a line of black liquid fills the cup. He lifts the plastic window, retrieves the coffee, and turns to find a table, spotting a man sitting alone, reading a book about woodcraft. "I actually have that book in my workshop right now," John says, approaching the man.

The man, around John's age, looks up. "No kidding! I've made a few things, but I'm basically a beginner."

"Me, too," John says.

The man points to the bench across from him. "You're welcome to join me." John sits and the man extends his hand. "I'm Larry."

John shakes his hand. "John. So, what all have you made? Do you have your own shop?"

Larry laughs. "Well, I call it my shop. My wife calls it the garage. Someday, I hope to live in a place that will allow me to have a shop out back. I've made a couple of end tables that would never win any prizes, but they're functional. I'm reading about how to make a kitchen table. How about you?"

John scratches his head. "Um, I seemed to bypass starting off by making end tables and went directly from making picture frames to making a kitchen table." Larry smiles, listening. "I had hoped to have it done by October and then I moved it to Thanksgiving, but now, I don't know."

Larry notices as John's face darkens and says, "So, what are you here for? Are things okay?"

John looks at the table and clears his throat. "My wife had part of a lung removed three days ago. Cancer."

"I'm sorry to hear that. Have the doctors told you anything?"

"They don't seem to have much good to say right now. It started out as breast cancer a couple of months ago and it spread."

Quiet engulfs the table, and for a moment John wishes he hadn't sat down. "Doctors don't always get it right," Larry says. "Forty years ago, they gave my mother two months to live. She just celebrated her seventy-second birthday."

John looks up at him. "What happened?"

Larry shakes his head, trying to put it into words. "I'm not a minister or a pastor or a chaplain. I'm just a man that looks at a piece of wood and knows it comes from a tree and realizes that we haven't been able to create a seed, let alone a tree. From that tree we're able to make homes, furniture, wagons, boats, and whatever else. I know that when I blink that man can't create anything to match that." He folds his hands on the table and looks down at them. "So, my mother got sick and we prayed to God, who said He created the trees. Our church prayed. Family from all over prayed. And we left the prayers with God." John listens to him with interest. "But we had also prayed for my grandfather, who died at sixty just a year earlier." John's face clouds over. "All I know is God is big enough and powerful enough to create a tree and a seed and big enough to restructure a damaged heart and get rid of cancer cells. I believe that, John. I really do. I don't know why that happens for some people and not others. I don't know why my grandpa died and my mother lived. But when people are sick, I pray for them because that's what I can do. I leave the rest to God and however He sees fit to heal . . . or not heal here on earth."

They sit in silence for several moments. "We don't go to church," John says. "I went some with my grandparents when I was little, and I actually did believe in God . . . I

∂o believe in God. And for some strange reason, I believe in Him even more now because of Joan's cancer. And for the first time I tried praying. I don't think I did it right, but I tried it."

Larry nods. "I thank God. Honor Him. I ask for His forgiveness and for help and direction for myself and others. I'm just talking and listening. That's praying, as far as I know."

"What if you don't get what you ask for?"

"Then that's my answer," Larry says. "Believing God hears prayer is faith. Then you wait." John looks at him, curious. "It takes strength to wait. That's the hardest part. Some people wait decades. A lifetime. My mother still prays for my brother, who's a lost and wandering soul. Some people die and long after they're gone the prayers they prayed for somebody are finally answered. It's not a magic trick."

John nods, looking at the table. "I wish it was. I wish Joan could hop out of that bed healthy and strong right now."

"I wish that, too." Larry pauses and looks at him. "When my mother got sick, even though I was a kid, I never looked at things the same way after that. Still don't. I didn't like it at the time. I hated it. It was an awful, gut-wrenching time. She didn't get better right away; it took a couple of years. It was years for all of us, waiting and praying, getting mad, crying, believing and then not believing, and then believing again, but I don't look at people the same way. I don't look at situations the same way." His eyes get misty as he thinks about it. "I'd hate to go back and do all of that over, but I would." He stops, looking out over the cafeteria and then back at John. "I never thought about that before, but I would."

"You got that kind of faith from looking at a piece of wood?" John says.

Larry's mouth turns up a bit, smiling.

Joan opens her eyes to see John sitting next to her hospital bed. She reaches for his hand and he looks up, noticing that she is awake, and stands next to her bed, holding her hand. "I didn't know if I would be able to breathe as well with part of a lung missing," she says. "But each time I wake up, I realize that I'm still breathing."

He leans down to kiss her. "I've been watching you breathe for the last three days."

She shakes her head. "Sounds boring." He chuckles and she squeezes his hand. "Go home, John. Go to work. You don't need to be here with me all the time. Go home to the kids."

"Your parents are with the kids, and they are having a great time. The kids don't miss me, trust me! Gigi said your mom made caramel corn yesterday. How can I compete with caramel corn?" He pats her hand and sits on the side of her bed. "If you're up for it, maybe your parents can bring the kids to see you today."

She looks up at the ceiling. "We need to talk about what Dr. Levy said."

He shakes his head, looking at her. "Doctors aren't always right. Dr. Kim said that herself to you. I met a man in the cafeteria who said the same thing."

She manages a smile and squeezes his hand. "Things don't look good, John."

He bites the inside of his lip, thinking. "Not to them. But we're not them, Joan." Her eyes are full of love, looking at him. He wants to believe, and she can't squash that, knowing that the time will come when he will be left with no other option but to face the reality of their situation. "We're fighters," he says. "We fight through things. We do what the doctors tell us, and we will pray, leaving it with God."

She looks at him, wondering what has shifted his thinking like this in the last few weeks. "Okay, John," she says, not fully believing, but seeing the belief in his eyes seems to make her stronger, if even for this moment.

FIFTEEN

September 2012

Lauren drives out of Grandon and into the country, following the directions on her cell phone. Teresa, a longtime friend of Gloria, is donating a week's stay at her Florida condo for the annual Glory's Place fund-raiser in December. The condo is situated right on the beach and pulls in a lot of money during the auction each year. The entire staff and volunteers begin collecting donations as early as the summer. Lauren notices a farm as she drives to Teresa's and realizes that she has never been on this particular road before. She turns and heads up the long drive to the farm, wondering out loud what she is doing. A modest two-story home is on the left and a small white barn sits to the right with a larger red barn behind it. A yellow Labrador retriever runs from behind the house, wagging his tail as he greets Lauren, who is opening the car door.

"Hi," a middle-aged woman says, opening the front door. "Can I help you?"

Lauren smiles at her. "Well, I'm not sure, but I hope so. I'm trying to find a dairy farmer named Bud."

The woman walks down the steps of the home to her, petting the top of the dog's head as she walks. "A farmer named Bud?" Lauren nods. "I don't know a farmer by that name, but let's ask my husband. Come back this way." She leads Lauren toward the red barn and begins to wave her arms and shout out her husband's name when she sees him leaving the barn driving a tractor. "Jason!" she yells, running so she can get in his line of vision. "Jason!" A man around forty, wearing jeans and a short-sleeve work shirt, sees his wife and turns off the tractor.

"What's up?" he says, noticing Lauren and taking his ball cap off to scratch his head.

"This woman is trying to find a dairy farmer named Bud. Do you know him?"

He gets off the tractor and stands in front of them. "Bud?"

Lauren nods, smiling. "I'm so sorry to bother you. You didn't have to stop your work."

"It's always here," he says, sticking a hand in his jeans pocket. "You say he's a dairy farmer?"

"I think so. He sells milk. Or at least he used to sell milk."

"The Coys sell milk," his wife says, thinking out loud.

Jason nods. "They do. They haven't been farming long. Maybe five years. But nobody there is named Bud as far as I know. Has Bud been farming long?" he asks, looking at Lauren.

"I think so. I don't know for sure, but I think it's been several years."

"The Hermans have been farming for years. Corn and soybeans. But they have sold milk in the past. They have a few cows on their farm. They don't sell in stores. Just on their farm. I don't think there's anybody named Bud there, either, but you could stop and ask."

Lauren raises her hand over her eyes to keep from squinting. "Thanks so much! Where is the Herman farm?"

Jason points west. "Stay on this road headed west for four miles until you come to Glade. Do you know where that is?" Lauren shakes her head. "You can't miss it. There's a flashing yellow light and a small antiques shop on the right. Turn left onto Glade and about three miles up on the right you'll see what's left of a crop of corn. The house, the barn, and the silos sit back off the road, like ours. You can't miss it. Jim Herman owns it."

Lauren extends her hand. "Thank you so much. Again, so sorry to bother you."

He shakes his head. "No bother." He smiles. "If it's organic milk you're wanting, Clauson's and other grocery stores carry it."

She smiles. "I'm actually not wanting the milk. I'm hoping Bud can help me find somebody."

September 1972

Joan sits at the kitchen table and riffles through the recipe box filled with recipes from her mother. She is wearing a bright, multicolored scarf around her head; her arms are slender sticking out of her shirt and her fingers are bony, but she wants to cook. Friends and family have been so kind to bring meals to them following her surgery, but she can't bear to look at one more casserole. She and John have secretly called the meals "hospital food," because it was all given to them following her stay in the hospital and the thought of eating one more hospital meal nearly takes her appetite away. The surgery was nearly three weeks ago and little by little she is regaining strength and wants to cook again.

When she first came home, Gigi and Christopher

would play atop her bed or on the floor of her bedroom to be near her. As Joan's strength returns, she lies on the sofa as the children play in the living room, drifting in and out of sleep. Each day before work and before going to bed each evening, John sits on the edge of the bed and holds Joan's hand. "Thank you, God, for what you're doing inside Joan's body today," he says. "Thank you for making her strong." She still isn't sure what to think about this, but it can't hurt, and John seems to believe in a way that she can't quite wrap her mind around.

She finds a recipe for white chicken chili, one of her favorites as a child growing up, and begins to look over the card. *How we all love this white chicken chili!* Her mother wrote. *Remember the trip we took out west one summer and we ordered this at a restaurant that exclaimed, "Voted best white chicken chili ten years in a row!" You finished your bowl and said, "The people who voted for this obviously don't have any taste buds. Yours is much better, Mom!" How many meals did we eat around our kitchen table together? How many arguments did we get in? How many tears did we wipe off our cheeks from laughing? How many problems did we solve? I can't imagine what our lives would've been like without those mealtimes. No matter what you're going through, always come back to the table with your family.*

Tears fill Joan's eyes as she reads her mother's writing, and she sighs with the disappointment in not taking an interest in cooking until a few months earlier. Christopher is too young to remember this time in the kitchen with her, but will Gigi? She looks over her shoulder and calls, "Kids, do you want to help me cook?" She can hear Gigi rustling to her feet in the living room.

"Are you cooking today, Mommy?" The little girl asks, looking at her from the hallway.

Joan holds up the recipe card. "White chicken chili!"

Gigi runs to the kitchen and Christopher toddles after her. "Are you feeling better?" Gigi asks, putting her hands on her mom's leg and looking up at her.

Joan squeezes Gigi's cheeks, kissing her forehead and then Christopher's. "Just thinking about your grandma's white chicken chili makes me feel better!"

"Mommy?" Gigi's face is turned up and her eyes are wide.

"Yeah, babe?"

"Can you breathe?"

Joan smiles. "Can I breathe? I'm talking to you, so that means I'm breathing."

"But is your breathing in half? And will it go down all the way someday?"

Joan realizes what Gigi is asking and pulls her close to her. "I will say that breathing feels different from what I'm used to, and I probably won't be running any marathons, but that's okay because I hate running anyway, but I'm breathing just fine."

"And white chicken chili helps?"

"It helps and your dad helps, and you and Christopher especially help!"

Gigi smiles, wrapping her arms around her mom.

SIXTEEN

September 2012

After Lauren picks up the paperwork for the free condo rental in Florida for the Glory's Place fundraiser, she makes her way to the Herman farm, hoping to remember the directions. She turns left at the flashing caution light and slows down when she sees what remains of a large corn crop. Turning in to the drive, she wonders again if all of this is worth it. No dog greets her here and no one seems to be home when she knocks on the front door. She walks down the stairs of the porch and around the house, toward the barns on the property, waving when she sees a man carrying a bucket of tools.

"Hiya!" he says, setting the bucket down.

Lauren picks up her pace to get closer to him. "Are you Jim?"

"I am," he says. He looks to be around forty-five with

a stocky frame and blond, brush-cut hair. "What can I do for you?"

She stops when she's a couple of feet away from him. "I'm hoping to find a dairy farmer named Bud."

Jim shakes his head and his mouth turns down as he thinks. "I don't know a Bud. A dairy farmer?"

She nods. "I think so."

He keeps shaking his head as if the name or face will come to him. "I'm sorry. I don't know him. But if you want fresh milk, we do sell it."

Lauren smiles. "I'd love to buy some!"

He leads her to a small white building with a few refrigerators inside. "Two percent or whole?"

She thinks for a second. "One of each. I want to make yogurt again and use fresh, farm milk this time."

He pulls a gallon of each from the refrigerator and sets them on a table. "Ten dollars." She hands him the money and he turns back to the refrigerator, pulling out a Ziploc bag of shucked corn. "For you. On the house, or . . . on the farm."

She reaches for the bag. "Thanks so much!"

He looks at her. "Does Bud sell something other than milk that you're looking for?"

"I'm actually hoping he can help me find somebody."

He lifts both gallons of milk off the table and walks with her to her car. "I can ask my wife when she gets home. Her family has been here forever. If she's ever heard of him, I can let you know."

Lauren writes her phone number on a piece of scrap paper she finds in her car and adds, "If you lose that, you can just call Glory's Place and ask for the pregnant lady."

"Will do," Jim says, handing the gallons of milk to her. "And congratulations! We have four."

"I'm not sure I can handle one, let alone four," Lauren says, closing her car door.

"You'll be amazed what you can do," he says.

"Thanks for the corn!" she says as she turns her car around in the driveway.

Arriving home, Lauren removes a Ziploc bag of chicken pieces she had rubbed with spices and refrigerated that morning. She places the chicken pieces on a plate and picks up the recipe card, reading the ingredients for white barbecue sauce. Lauren reads the recipe: *Our friend June in Alabama gave me this recipe when your dad and I were first married. It's delicious on these grilled chicken pieces, pulled pork, even as sauce for coleslaw. When you find something you love, you stick with it. Guess that explains why your dad and I are still married! This is just exceptionally yummy!* Lauren smiles reading the words and opens a cabinet to find the mayonnaise.

She mixes the mayonnaise, apple cider vinegar, horse-radish, and fresh lemon juice with several seasonings and then dips her finger in for a taste. "Mmm. She's right. This is exceptionally yummy."

When Travis arrives home, Lauren is on the back deck as she finishes grilling the chicken pieces. She has made a spinach salad that she found among the recipes inside the table and read on the internet how to boil the perfect ear of corn. The table is set with new place mats, a simple woven fabric with hints of gray and blue, and a small ivory-colored vase filled with hydrangea flowers from the shrub at the corner of their house; both items were found during a trip with Miriam and Gloria to Hidden Treasures, the local thrift store. She places the food on the table and steps into the living room, calling up the stairs to Travis. He always takes a shower when he arrives home after a day of mowing and weeding park grounds and maintaining baseball and football fields. "What is this?" he says, looking at the meal on the table.

"More recipes from the cards we found," she says, smiling.

He wraps his arms around her, kissing her. "Our baby's mom is the best cook in all of Grandon!" They sit down and she waits for Travis to take a bite of the chicken. "Mmm. So good! You made this?"

She smiles. "I did! The recipe cards are teaching me."

"Man, am I ever glad you found those cards!"

"I actually tried to track down the owner of the cards today."

Travis lifts the cob of corn and takes a bite. He points the ear of corn at her. "Wow! Delicious. What do you mean you tried to track down the owner?"

"Whoever wrote the cards has mentioned a farmer named Bud a few times. I stopped at a couple of farms today to see if there was a Bud. I got the corn and some milk from one of the farms."

"Any luck?" Lauren shakes her head. "You really think someone is missing the cards?"

Lauren nods. "I do. They're not just recipes. They are family stories and memories. This family was close. I think these recipes are part of their legacy." She looks at him. "These cards were passed down to someone who was loved very much."

He stops eating, smiling. "Then let's find Bud!"

"Together?"

"When I was a kid, I wanted to be a detective. I was going to change my name to Burt Grimes."

She laughs out loud. "Burt Grimes! Why?"

"Because Detective Burt Grimes sounds like a detective," he says, as if she should know that. "It rhymes with crimes. Mabrey is soft. Weak. Come on!" He is genuinely perplexed that she can't figure this out on her own.

He shakes it off. "You know how many old guys work or have worked at the parks department? Some of them have lived in Grandon their whole lives. If there's ever been a farmer named Bud, one of those guys knows him or his family."

"And yet another reason why I married you, Detective Grimes!"

SEVENTEEN

September 1972

Joan stands alongside John in his workshop, looking at the second table leg. He shakes his head. "Measure twice. Cut once." He sighs, aggravated. "I know that. I tell myself that all the time. But what did I do?"

"You measured once and cut twice?" Joan asks, confused.

"I measured once and cut. Period." He lifts up the other leg that he finished weeks ago. "Look at them! Not even close to looking alike."

Joan cocks her head, looking at each leg. "They look exactly the same, John."

He snaps his head to look at her. "Are you kidding?"

She laughs, looking at the legs. "John! These legs are identical."

"Really? Then why is this one an eighth of an inch wider than this one?"

She looks at him, dumbfounded. "An eighth of an inch? Who's going to notice that? It's going to be *under* the table. I can't even notice it and I'm standing right here in front of them."

He holds each of the two table legs directly in front of himself, shaking his head. "You can't see what I'm seeing." A thought dawns on him and he looks at Joan, setting the legs down on the worktable, thinking. "That's how it is, isn't it?" She's not sure if he's talking to her or himself. "Right?"

"What do you mean? How what is?" she says.

He puts his hands on top of his head, realizing. "You can't see the difference."

"I know. We've covered this."

He looks at her, wide-eyed. "We can't *see* the difference inside of you." She stares at him. "We don't know what's *happening* inside of—"

"We do know, John. The doctor—"

He cuts her off. "But we don't know what God is doing. We can't see the difference that He's making."

She sighs, her mouth turning down into a small, sad smile.

"Just listen to me, Joan. I made those table legs. I can see the difference between them, but you can't. If God made your body, and I believe He did, do you?" She nods. "Then He can see what's happening inside your lungs and your breasts and your body. He can see the difference from day one of your cancer diagnosis to today."

Joan is struggling to understand him. "What kind of difference?"

"He's *doing* something that we can't see."

He needs to stop this way of thinking. "John, you're talking a miracle and . . ."

He puts one of his hands on each side of her face. "Joan, I wouldn't say it if I didn't believe it, would I?" She pauses and then shakes her head. "God's doing something and even if we don't see it, even if you don't feel it yet, He sees the difference inside of you."

Her eyes get misty looking at him. "I want to believe, John, but . . ."

"I believe," he says, pulling her to him.

She pulls back to look at him. "How?"

He reaches for a piece of wood, smiling. "This." He smiles and kisses her. "Today's the day. God's doing something. Today's the day."

September 2012

Lauren and Stacy each take a bite of chess pie inside Gloria's office and smile at her. "Scrumptious, right?" Gloria says.

Stacy nods, chewing. "Delicious. I wonder if the person leaving these goodies is trying to bribe you?"

"Bribe me?" Gloria says, clutching her chest. "Why would anyone bribe *me*?"

"Maybe you have a gentleman suitor," Lauren says, grinning. "Maybe a handsome stranger is trying to bribe your love away from Marshall."

Gloria laughs. "Oh, that's absurd!" She pauses a moment. "Or is it? You know, when I was younger, I really was quite fetching."

"Isn't 'fetching' a word that's generally associated with canines, Gloria?" Miriam says, entering the office. Gloria shakes her head in annoyance. "Why do you continue to try to figure out who's doing this?" she says, putting a slice of pie onto a small paper plate. "Isn't it obvious?" Stacy, Lauren, and Gloria shake their heads and shrug. "It's Larry."

"Larry the furniture maker?" Lauren says. "Why him, of all people?"

Miriam smiles, taking a bite of pie. "He's always been a bit smitten."

"With me?" Gloria says, shocked and nearly choking on her bite of pie.

"Of course not!" Miriam says coyly. "With me."

"He's married," Lauren says. "For like, forty-some years, right?"

"There's always been a hint of flirtation," Miriam says, taking another bite of her pie and sighing with delight.

Lauren looks at Gloria, who is using her index finger to circle her ear, and Lauren chuckles. "Miriam, I didn't notice anything when we were at Larry's together. As a matter of fact, he paid more attention to me than he did you." Gloria coughs, choking on a bite of pie. "I think you're reading way too much into everyday conversation." Miriam's eyes are wide with dismay. "If it was Larry, he'd drop off a wooden box or bowl, not food!"

The office is quiet, and Stacy and Gloria exchange glances before bursting into laughter. "Oh, shut up, Gloria!" Miriam says, reaching for another piece of pie.

"Well, if you'd said Jerry at Clauson's, that would have made sense," Gloria says. "He's the bakery manager. But Larry the wood guy?" She thinks for a moment. "It could be Jerry! The last time we were in there together, he looked at you and said, 'What can I get you, ma'am?' If that's not innuendo, I don't know what is!" Miriam opens her mouth to argue with Gloria as Stacy and Lauren leave the office, ready to greet the kids for the day with Andrea, who is entering the front door.

"There's fresh pie in Gloria's office," Lauren says.

Andrea grabs a piece and walks with Lauren out the front doors to wait for the children on the sidewalk. "So," she says, taking a bite. "Who do you think is leaving the goodies?"

Lauren shrugs. "I just hope they don't stop making deliveries. Did you cook with your kids when they were growing up?"

Andrea puckers her mouth, thinking. "Some. They were always so busy with sports and other after-school activities that I usually had dinner ready when they got home."

"Was dinner important?"

Andrea looks at Lauren's face. She's so sincere about this and realizes, from what Lauren said about her childhood, that she wants to do the opposite of what her own mother did. "All the meals were important." She takes another bite, watching the traffic at the stoplight in front of the building. "When the kids were little, we ate breakfast and dinner together with Bill. And when they got so busy as teens, we *still* ate breakfast and dinner together. Sometimes it meant that we ate at four thirty, before a game, or at eight thirty, after a game, but we made sure that we came together at those meals." The first car makes its way up the driveway. "Do you and Travis like to cook?"

Lauren nods, opening the car door for seven-year-old Evan. "I'm trying to learn but yeah, we get in the kitchen together a lot."

Andrea helps Brianna and Jacob from a car, smiling at them. "You could have your own cooking class here," she says. "I bet Brianna and Jacob would love to learn how to bake cookies!" The kids hoot and cheer at the word "cookies," and Lauren smiles at the thought.

EIGHTEEN

October 1972

J oan reaches for a scarf of autumn browns, oranges, yellows, and reds and ties it around her head in the bathroom, looking at herself in the mirror. Besides the sickness following each round of chemo, looking at herself has been the hardest part of cancer. Her skin is pale, her hair is gone, the flesh on her body seems to rest closer to bone each week, and her eyes stare out from dark, hollowed-out holes. Her eyes fill with tears at the sight of herself, but when she hears Gigi's and Christopher's voices from the kitchen, she reaches for a tissue from the box on the counter, pressing it to each eye. She listens to her kids chatter for a moment and takes a deep breath, looking at herself again. "Today's the day," she whispers, surprising herself. The words plant themselves somewhere deep inside and once again, tears spring to her eyes. "Today's the day," she says, exhaling.

John enters the bathroom wearing his work uniform and smiles at her. "The kids are eating breakfast. I need to get to a woman's house by eight. Fridge on the fritz." He puts his hands on her shoulders. "Wow! Are you ever beautiful!" She shakes her head. "Crazy kind of beautiful."

She laughs. "You're the crazy one, John Creighton."

"Today's the day. Right?"

She smiles, nodding. "Today's the day," she says.

John thrusts his fist into the air. "Yes!" He kisses her good-bye and promises to call on his break.

She follows John to the kitchen and reaches for a skillet as he says good-bye to the kids; she wants to get at least a couple of meals prepared today before she goes in for chemotherapy tomorrow. While Gigi and Christopher eat some scrambled eggs, fruit, and toast that John made them, Joan pulls out two pounds of ground beef from the refrigerator. "What are you making, Mommy?" Gigi asks from the table.

"Chili."

The little girl raises her head higher. "With little corn muffins?"

"I can do that," Joan says, breaking apart the beef inside the skillet with a wooden spoon.

"I can help when I finish," Gigi says. "I need to eat for strength." Joan laughs. How many times has Gigi heard John or her mom, Alice, say those words to Joan over the last three months? "Have you eaten for strength today yet, Mommy?"

Joan laughs again. "No, I haven't."

Gigi's face straightens like a prosecutor's inside a courtroom. "Eat for strength now before you get weak!"

Joan raises her hands in surrender. "I know, I know. I'll do that before I start the chili. I don't know what I was thinking."

"You weren't thinking," Gigi says, taking a huge bite of toast.

Joan laughs again and reaches into the fridge for an egg to scramble for herself, along with some leftover salad from dinner last night. It sounds horrible to the rest of her family, but for some reason Joan has been craving greens and nuts and eats them throughout the day, even at breakfast. She sits down at the table to eat and smiles, watching Christopher maneuver his tiny fork, using it as a mini shovel to scoop up a piece of egg, which falls to the plate, but he perseveres, trying again until a bite reaches his mouth. "What a big boy!" she says, reaching over the table to squeeze his hand. The thought invades her brain that she won't hear Christopher string a sentence together or run the bases at the local ball field, but as quickly as it comes, she shoots it down. "Today's the day," she says, looking at Christopher and then Gigi.

"For what?" Gigi asks.

"To believe," Joan says. "Like Daddy."

Gigi grins. "He says that a lot," she says, happy to be sitting here at the table with her mom and baby brother. "Because it will make you strong."

Joan thinks for a moment. "Saying it won't necessarily make me strong. Daddy believes that saying it will create faith and help us believe."

"In what?" Gigi asks, finishing her eggs.

Joan moves her own eggs around the plate, not wanting to eat them. "In what we can't see."

"Like the wind," Gigi says, shoving the last of the toast in her mouth and then showing it to Christopher, making him giggle.

Joan puts her fork down, looking at Gigi, taken aback by what she's said. "Like the wind," she whispers, watching Gigi and Christopher as they each open their mouths full of food. She's never thought much about the wind, but without giving it a moment's thought, her five-year-old daughter has touched on something unseen but real. "We see what it touches," she says.

"What *what* touches?" Gigi asks, reaching for her milk.

"You're so brilliant and amazing!" Joan says, adoring her daughter and son. "You both are!"

"Why?" Gigi says, tipping the cup to her mouth again.

"Because you said we can't see the wind! We can't *see* the wind, but we see what it touches, don't we? The trees, the grass, flags, lakes, our hair . . . or at least your hair," Joan says, chuckling.

"Our ball when it's in the yard," Gigi says, joining in. "Our faces and umbrellas and . . . what else?"

Joan opens her arms. "Everything! The wind touches everything outside, and when our windows are open, it touches our curtains and things inside the house!" She props her arm on the table, resting her chin on her hand. "Like I said, you're brilliant!"

Gigi smiles and says, "What does it mean?"

Joan rears her head back, laughing. "It means, today's the day! We may not be able to see God, but just like the wind we can see what He touches, right?"

Gigi shrugs. "Yes!"

Joan takes a bite of her egg and marvels at what has just happened. Was it just a cute-kid moment? Or did God use Gigi to speak this simple—but what Joan believes is a profound—truth, to her? Six months ago, Joan would have believed it was a sweet, funny-kid instance, but today? Today she ponders if God uses the smallest, most mundane moments of the day to speak to us. She'll have to think more about that and figure out what she believes. She takes another bite of egg and lifts the recipe for her mom's chili out of the recipe box. *How many bowls of this chili did we eat throughout the years? I always made it on the days we went sledding. Remember that morning we went sledding at Grandma and Grandpa's and you broke your arm? It was so windy that day!* Joan rereads the words: *It was so windy that day!* She stares at the words. Of all the recipes to choose, she picked this one that describes the wind on that long-ago day. Can this be chalked up to coincidence or is God repeating or clarifying something for her? She shakes her head, not really knowing what to believe, and keeps reading.

We wrapped scarves around our faces, but the wind was blowing right through them! It was so strong! In the emergency room you said, "There better be a bowl of chili left when I get home!" You weren't concerned about your arm, just the chili! This is the recipe I made for your sixth-grade Halloween party. I made two huge pots and they both came home empty. I remember so many of those kids said they'd never eaten chili before. That made me so sad because I just couldn't imagine a home without a huge pot of chili. I always mixed the kind of beans I'd use: chili beans, kidney beans, red beans, and black beans. I loved making it and boy, did all of you love eating it! When you were a teen, I had to use three or four pounds of ground beef because you loved it as leftovers. And yes, on that cold, windy day when you broke your arm, there was a pot of chili waiting for you! Chili makes your house smell great when it's cooking, and there's nothing like coming home from school to the smell of dinner cooking on the stove. At least that's what you always told me! That's still a favorite memory for Joan: coming home from school and flinging open the back door to the smells of cookies, rolls, cakes, casseroles, bread, chicken, or beef baking inside the oven, or a pot of soup simmering on the stove. She looks back down at the recipe. *I didn't have a lot of skills, but I could cook and I'm glad I could because I still remember the times we spent around the table together. I believe it makes families closer. I really do!* Joan smiles at the four smiley faces her mother drew at the bottom of the card.

After she puts the last bite of salad into her mouth, she gets up, smiling at the kids. "So, who's helping me?" Gigi bounces out of her chair and Christopher turns as far around as he can in the high chair, looking for her. "Come on, big guy," Joan says, lifting him out and getting a kiss from him. "Let's make the house smell good!"

October 2012

It isn't as easy as Travis thought it would be to find someone who recognizes the name of Bud the farmer. No one at the parks department recognizes the name, and he dreads telling Lauren that in his search, he has only hit dead ends. He is using a leaf blower around the gazebo in the Grandon town square when he notices Robert Layton waving at him. Robert's law office sits on the square, just two doors down from Marshall's Department Store, and Travis's family has known Robert and his family for as long as Travis can remember. He turns off the leaf blower as Robert steps toward him. "I haven't seen you since I've heard the news," Robert says. "Congratulations!"

Travis takes off his Grandon Parks Department hat and wipes his forehead. "Thanks!"

"When is Lauren due?"

"In December."

Robert nods, smiling. "A baby for Christmas. Fantastic! Is Lauren doing well? If I get home this evening and Kate learns that I've neglected to ask all the pertinent questions, I'll never hear the end of it."

Travis chuckles. "She's doing great. She's taking time to do some decorating in the house and get the room ready for the baby and is learning to cook." A thought strikes him, and he interrupts Robert as he's about to ask another question. "Hey, Robert! You don't happen to know a farmer named Bud, do you?"

Robert shields his eyes from the sun as he looks at him. "Bud Waters?"

Travis's eyes light up. "Really? There *is* a farmer named Bud?"

Robert nods. "A dairy farmer." Travis beams at the words. "He sold the farm fifteen or twenty years ago."

The smile leaves Travis's face. "Do you know where he lives now?"

Robert looks up to the sky, thinking. "Drake County, I think. It's been a lot of years to remember. Why?"

"Lauren really wants to find him. Hoping he can help her find somebody else."

"Well, let me poke around. If I find him, I'll let you know ASAP."

"That's great, Robert! Thanks. What can we do for you for helping us?"

"Name the baby after me," Robert says, walking toward his office. Travis laughs, but as he starts the leaf blower again, he looks at Robert's back as he walks away, wondering if he was serious.

NINETEEN

October 1972

Joan sits in one of the chairs in the chemo room at the cancer clinic as the chemo drips through the IV line and into her arm. There are two other chairs inside this room; the chair next to her is empty, but the one near the door is taken. A young man around twenty or so sits in the chair, and a woman who Joan believes is his mother sits next to him; her hand is on his arm, and Joan thinks of her own mom at home with Gigi and Christopher.

Joan's father brought her to the clinic today so John would not miss another day of work. On her insistence, her dad has gone to find a bowl of soup in the cafeteria for her. If they don't have broccoli cheese—and she knows the cafeteria will not—she has instructed him where a nearby café that makes it is located. She has sent her father on a scavenger hunt of sorts because he is never able to hide his concern, and Joan knows it is best if she receives the chemo alone. As the cancer killer drips through the IV, Joan whispers again, "Today's the day. I may not see it, but God is at work." Her mind wanders ahead to Halloween, and she wonders if she'll be up for walking Gigi and Christopher around the neighborhood. Her mom found a lion costume a couple of months ago at a sale for Christopher, complete with a golden, bushy mane to frame his face. Gigi has said she wants to be Big Bird from *Sesame Street,* but Joan questions whether she can make the costume. She closes her eyes to rest and seems to be drifting toward sleep when she hears "Today's the day. God is working. I just know it."

Joan flashes her eyes open and looks at the mother and her son, but they aren't in conversation. The young man's eyes are closed, and the mother is reading. "Did you say something?" Joan asks, keeping her voice low.

The woman, who looks to be in her late forties, with short blond hair and a stout figure, turns to see Joan. "I'm so sorry," she says, whispering. "I didn't mean to say it out loud."

Joan lifts her head from the back of the chair, wanting to come out of it altogether. "What did you say?" Her voice is earnest, almost pleading.

The woman looks at her son and gets up from her

chair, stepping gingerly to Joan and whispers, "I said, today's the day."

"You did say it!" Joan puts a hand to her head and looks at the chair next to her. "Could you sit down?" The woman does and Joan gropes for words. "Why did you say that?"

The woman shrugs, her eyes lighting up as she talks. "Bruce was diagnosed with cancer two months ago. For some reason, on the day he was diagnosed, I said, 'Today's the day. God is working.'"

Joan looks at her, puzzled. "What did you mean by that?"

"I knew that we could be scared to death and start wringing our hands or we could pound our stake firmly into the ground and believe that God is at work, not tomorrow or the next day, but today, right now."

Joan feels tears begin to swell and she shakes her head to keep them from falling. "My husband has been saying those same words to me." The woman's eyes open wide as she listens. "And now you. The same words! Isn't that strange?"

The woman smiles. "Do you think it's coincidence?"

Joan looks into the woman's blue eyes; they aren't condescending but are full of kindness. "Part of me thinks that it is, but another part wonders."

"Wonders what?"

Joan looks up at the ceiling and back at the woman. "If God is trying to get my attention? I thought that if He did that it'd be something bigger like a meteor shower, not something like a sentence my husband is saying. Or the word 'wind' in a recipe!" The woman looks confused. "You had to be there." The woman laughs, understanding exactly what Joan is saying. "I'm not much of a believer." Joan stops, clarifying. "I mean, I believe in God, that's pretty much where it ends."

The woman puts her hand on Joan's arm. "Belief has to start somewhere. Your beginning is cancer. My beginning was my college fiancé dumping me our senior year. One of the best things that ever happened to me."

Joan's eyes fill with fear and she fights the urge to cry. "How can cancer be the best thing? What if . . ."

The woman nods, looking at her son. "I've gone through all the what-ifs. I know what could happen. My husband and I have talked about all of them. But what if the what-ifs don't happen?" Her eyes are sincere as she looks at Joan. "What if there is something greater than all of our what-ifs? What if God heals Bruce? What if He heals you? What if today *is* the day?"

The woman smiles and Joan feels tears in her eyes again. What if?

October 2012

Gloria, Miriam, and Lauren carry sections of a baby crib up the stairs and into the first bedroom on the right. Travis and Andrea follow, carrying a small white chest of drawers. Gloria spotted the crib, complete with mattress, pads, sheets, and chest of drawers at a garage sale and called Lauren right away. She insisted that she and Marshall buy the items for the baby's room. "You're going to have a baby shower anyway, so consider these your first and probably best gifts!" Gloria said.

Travis works at putting the crib together as the women place the chest of drawers against the wall, next to the door. Miriam looks around the small room. "You're going to need a chair or rocking chair of some sort there in the corner."

Lauren looks at the empty space. "You think?"

"If you breast-feed in the middle of the night," Andrea says, "a chair is nice in the baby's room." She looks around the room. "I remember Bill and I doing this like it was yesterday."

"Me, too," Gloria says. "The days were long, but the years were short." Miriam and Andrea nod in agreement, smiling at Lauren.

"That just means there will be days that will feel like

they'll never end, but they do," Andrea says. "And it feels like the years fly by, and they do."

"Oh, to be a young mother again," Miriam says, pulling the crib sheets from the bag to be washed.

"Would you do it again, Miriam?" Lauren asks.

"She's too old to do it again," Gloria says.

"Says Grandma Moses," Miriam replies. "I'd do some things differently, and I can leave all those things in the hands of you and Travis, to do right what I got wrong."

"We're just thrilled to be grandmas again," Gloria says.

"She will be Grandma," Miriam says. "I will be Noni M."

Gloria scoffs. "How is it that even your grandma name annoys me?"

Lauren waves her hand at them to stop and positions Andrea next to them, in the middle of the room. "Say cheese," she says, holding up her phone to take a picture.

"Noni M!" Gloria says, making all of them laugh. She claps her hands together and says, "There are some miscellaneous pictures for the wall and a few baby toys I found at the sale in my car."

"Gloria, you didn't say—" Lauren begins.

"I couldn't resist," Gloria says. "They were inexpensive and cute and if you don't want them, there are plenty of parents at Glory's Place who can use them." Miriam and Andrea go with her to the car as Travis's cell phone rings. He notices it is Robert Layton's number.

"Hi, Robert!"

"Please tell Lauren that farmer Bud lives thirty miles from here."

Travis looks at Lauren and smiles.

TWENTY

October 1972

John uses a table saw to cut a new table leg to replace the one he miscut a couple of weeks ago. Although he has moved his finish date, at this rate, he worries that he will not have the table completed for Christmas. Fear pushes against his heart, and he wonders if Joan will be here at Christmas. He presses his fingers into his eyes in an effort to drive away the thought. "Today's the day," he says, his voice catching. Joan is getting thinner, and fatigue grips her many more times a day. "You're doing things I can't see," he whispers. He finishes the cut and stops the saw, putting his head down, too tired or too distracted to continue. "You're doing things I can't see," he whispers again, his lip beginning to quiver. He grips the workbench. "I believe." He closes his eyes against the tears. "But there's part of me that doesn't. Help me believe."

The door to his shop opens and John straightens, wiping his face before he turns around, and when he does, he laughs out loud. Christopher is wearing an adorable fluffy lion costume, and Gigi is smiling ear to ear in what looks like a hooded, velvety yellow rug with two eyes and a yellow cone nose pointing straight out.

"Grandma and Mommy finished my costume!" Gigi says. Joan smiles, looking at the kids.

"Where's Gigi?" John asks Joan.

"Daddy! Here!" Gigi says, laughing.

John looks shocked. "Here? I thought you were Big Bird!" He stands back. "Let me take a better look." He nods. "Yep, now I see that you are my Gigi, but when you came in . . ."

"I tricked you," Gigi says, pleased.

"Not just me. Every house you go to will be tricked!" He looks at Joan. "Great job!"

She picks up Christopher and says, "Roar for Daddy." The little boy opens his mouth and makes a noise that sounds more like a duck than a lion.

John laughs, poking Christopher in the belly. "So, tomorrow night, right?" he says, looking at Gigi.

She bounces her head up and down. "What will you and Mommy be?" Gigi asks.

"I'm going to go as a heat and A/C repairman," John says.

Gigi shakes her head. "That's your job! Your costume has to be pretend."

"If you ask any of my customers, many of them will say that I pretend to be a repairman." Joan laughs out loud and kisses Christopher's face.

Gigi looks up at Joan. "What about you, Mommy?"

"Um, I'm thinking I could borrow a gown from the hospital and go as a patient."

Gigi shakes her head. "No, Mommy. We see you as that all the time. You need to have a pretend costume."

Joan's face straightens at the words and she sets Christopher down. "That's how they see me," she says, looking at John. "As a patient. Somebody sick." She looks down at Gigi, who is trying to keep Christopher from taking off his lion hood.

"You are a patient, Joan. That's all she means."

"I don't want her to remember me as being sick and puny," she whispers hotly.

"Nobody said puny," John says.

"*I* said puny! Sick, puny, and whiny. I don't want any of it," Joan snaps.

Gigi and Christopher pop up their heads to look at Joan. "What's wrong, Mommy?" Gigi asks.

"Nothing's wrong," Joan says. "I'm just working on some costume ideas."

October 2012

Lauren and Travis spend time in the kitchen making a three-cheese egg casserole. She leans over, reading the recipe card on the counter: *Absolutely one of our favorites! Saturday mornings were made for this.* "When Grandma got *so sick that winter, you helped me make this for her and Gramps several times. How many meals did we take to them that winter? This dish always made Grandma smile. I hope it still makes you and your family smile, baby girl.*

Lauren puts eggs, milk, and sugar into a bowl and mixes them while Travis grates a cup of Monterey Jack cheese and cubes two ounces of cream cheese. "What if we don't find Bud?" she asks, reaching for the cottage cheese in the refrigerator. "Or what if we do find him and he has no idea who the cards belong to?"

Travis melts butter in the microwave. "If we're honest, it's a long shot." He picks up the recipe card. "Unless he recognizes the handwriting or has an exceptional memory of a customer who told him that they used his milk to make homemade yogurt, I'd say the chances of tracking down the owner of the cards are slim to none." He looks at her and knows he's disappointed her. "But anything's possible, right?"

Lauren adds the three cheeses and butter to the egg mixture, plus a half cup of flour and a teaspoon of baking powder. She mixes everything together and pours it into a three-quart baking dish, then opens the oven door, holding her belly as she does. When she straightens, her hand is still on her stomach, and she gasps. "The baby's kicking again!" She reaches for Travis's hand and puts it on the spot, making him smile.

"Feisty," he says, looking at her. "Just like his mom . . . or her mom!" He keeps his hand over the spot, and the baby kicks again, making him smile. "At least she doesn't give up like her dad."

Lauren puts her hand on top of his. "You're not giving up. You're being practical. And you're right. It is a long shot that Bud will know anything."

He pulls her to him, wrapping his arms around her. "But there is a slight chance. We're Mabreys, and we believe a slight chance is better than no chance at all!"

"Really?" Lauren says, looking at him.

He nods. "After all, there was a slight chance that you'd learn to cook and look what has happened!" She pulls away from him, grabs a dish towel from the counter, and swats him. "I love you," he says. "I think you're amazing." The words make her blush. She didn't hear words of praise growing up. Someday she hopes to receive a compliment without feeling awkward, but she knows that until then, Travis will continue to praise her. He bends over and looks at the casserole inside the oven. "I think *this* is going to be amazing!"

She walks to the table and picks up the recipe card, reading from it. *"This dish always made Grandma smile. I hope it still makes you and your family smile, baby girl."* She looks at him. "It's already made you smile." She taps the table. "It's kind of cool to think that whoever wrote these recipes probably served them on this table."

"And you can pass the recipes and the table on to our child." He stops for a moment. "A *copy* of the recipes. Not *our* copy of the recipes. Let's not let that happen again."

TWENTY-ONE

October 1972

John, Joan, Gigi, and Christopher sit at the table, finishing their dinner of beef stroganoff with noodles. The anticipation of the evening is about to make Gigi explode, and she wiggles in her seat. "When can I put on my costume?"

Joan laughs. "For the twentieth time, after you have warm food in your stomach. You can't just put candy in your belly."

"Yes, I could!" Gigi says in all seriousness, making John chuckle.

"I know you could," Joan says. "But I don't want you to get sick. I want you to have warm food in your stomach." Gigi begins to eat quickly, and Joan opens her mouth to stop her but gives up. Halloween comes around only once a year.

"So, you put warm food in *your* belly," Gigi says, "and then put your costume on."

"I've got it ready!" Joan says.

"You do?" John asks. "What is it?"

Joan smiles. "You'll see. I have one for you, too."

"Yay!" Gigi says, shoving another bite into her mouth before scrambling away from the table.

Christopher leans over his high chair, wanting down. "Okay, I give up," Joan says. "Are you full?" He nods. "Are you really full or do you just want to go get your costume on with Gigi?"

"Gigi," he says, looking for his sister.

Joan takes the bib from around his neck and lifts him from the high chair. "All right, let me hear your roar." Christopher opens his mouth like a baby bird and roars, sounding like a duck again and making Joan and John laugh together. She takes him to his bedroom and he quickly uses his tiny hands to remove his pants, sitting on the floor to finish kicking them off. Once his costume is on, Joan says, "Come on, big boy, let's go back to the kitchen." Christopher toddles after her and she leaves him with John, who's finishing his meal. Christopher reaches to get up on his lap in order to take a few more bites. Gigi bounds into the kitchen with her arms open wide, pieces of yellow cloth dangling down like bird feathers.

"Look at you!" John says.

"Let's go!" Gigi says, reaching for a plastic pumpkin bucket on the counter to collect candy.

"Wait for me!" Joan yells from the hallway. Minutes later, energetic music can be heard from the hallway as Joan enters the kitchen, holding the cassette player on top of one shoulder. She's wearing long, red satin shorts over white tights, a white T-shirt with the word CHAMP emblazoned across the front, boxing gloves, and a blue satin robe. She turns around so John can read what's on the back of it.

"Wrecking Ball," he says, pointing to the words for Gigi. And beneath those words he reads, "Champion 1972."

"You're a fighter!" Gigi squeals, thrilled with her mom's costume.

Joan throws John a shirt. "And I have Daddy's costume."

John holds the red shirt up and reads the word written in black paint across the back: "Trainer."

"This is the towel for over your shoulder," Joan says, throwing him a small, white towel. "No good trainer would get close to a ring without a towel."

John takes off his work shirt and pulls the other one over his head, tucks it into his pants, and throws the towel over his shoulder. "All right! Let me see what you've got. Show me some jabs." Joan jabs at the air.

"Head punch." She punches higher at an imaginary boxer. "High kicks," John barks.

Joan is about to do it but stops. "Kicking isn't legal. I'm a fair fighter."

"Not against your opponent," he says, smiling. "We need to kick its butt." He kisses her forehead, and Gigi grabs one of his hands.

"Come on! Let's go!"

"What about the mess?" Joan asks, looking at the table.

"I'll clean it later," John says, opening the garage door. "We've got a fight to get to!"

October 2012

When Lauren finishes her shift at Clauson's, she walks around the store, taking pictures of coworkers in their costumes. The store manager asked if she'd take several for the store's website and social media pages. In the floral department she snaps a picture of herself and Janie, who decided to dress as Dorothy to Lauren's Scarecrow from *The Wizard of Oz*. All Lauren needed was a hat, a stringy wig, and a big, ragged shirt and baggy pants to put over her pregnant belly to be the perfect scarecrow. At the front of the store, Ben is dressed as Gandalf from *The Lord of the Rings* and took the time to make pumpkin-shaped notes to put in the bags of customers who come through his line. Margie and Noel in the pharmacy are a princess and Luke Skywalker, and Greg and Tyson are an astronaut and Dracula in the meat department. She takes their picture together and is headed to the bakery when she sees Robert and Kate Layton dressed as a king and queen. "Robert! Or should I say, 'Your Highness.'" She curtsies to Kate. "Your Majesty."

Kate laughs. "It's the annual staff party. We're picking up the cake."

"Let me snap a picture." They pose for her, and she holds up her phone, capturing them. "Thanks again, Robert, for helping us find Bud. Travis and I are headed there as soon as I get out of this costume."

"Happy to help! Let me know how it goes."

Lauren looks at their picture as she walks to her car, hoping that she and Travis will still have a sense of fun when they're Robert and Kate's age. When she gets home, she takes off the costume and makeup and jumps in the car with Travis for the drive to Drake County. On arriving at what she hopes is Bud's home, Lauren rings the doorbell. There is no answer. She looks at the address at the side of the door again, making sure they are at the right place. She rings the doorbell again and waits. "I should have asked Robert if there was a phone number for Bud."

Travis tries to peer through the small window at the top of the door to see if he can spot anyone inside. Lauren looks at the door that isn't opening. "I guess I should leave a note?" He nods and she walks to the car for some paper. "All I have is a napkin!"

"It works," Travis says.

She thinks for a moment and writes, *Dear Bud, I hope you are the farmer who used to sell milk. I am trying to track someone down who used to be a customer of yours, and I'm hoping you can help.* She writes her phone number and her name and opens the storm door, letting it close against the note, leaving half of it sticking out. "Now the waiting game begins," she says.

"That's a horrible game," Travis says, walking to the car. "In the same category as the quiet game. Moms must have made up both those games."

She glares at him as she opens the passenger-side door. "I have a great idea, why don't *you* play the quiet game on the drive home?"

"See!" Travis says, sliding behind the wheel. "It's always the mom who suggests these awful games." Lauren giggles as he turns around in the driveway and heads for home.

TWENTY-TWO

November 1972

John tries to concentrate on making the third table leg. He never dreamed this project would take so long but knows that if he had more time in the shop, it would be nearly complete by now. He pushes the wood through the table saw and can hear the doctor's words in his head over the noise of the saw. "A setback." That's what Dr. Levy said a few days ago. Joan thought it was a virus at first. Her mom had been sick and there was word, as they're often is, that there was "something going around." But according to the doctor, this had nothing to do with any virus. "We found more cancer," Dr. Levy said. "You'll need another surgery to remove more of the lung." What little air there was in Joan's lung exhaled in despair. "I know this is a tremendous setback, Joan, but we need to remove it." Joan's eyes filled with tears. Not another

157

surgery. Not this close to Thanksgiving and Christmas. John grabbed her hand and looked at the doctor. "But I can't perform the surgery until you get your weight up." Joan glanced up at him. "You need to eat high-calorie, high-protein meals. Think cream, butter, steak, chicken, turkey, eggs, half-and-half, sour cream, cheese, olive oil," he said. "Do you cook?"

Joan tried to smile. "I've been learning, but all this has . . ."

"She does cook," John said. "She's a great cook."

"Good. Eat lots of veggies, especially tomatoes, carrots, onions, and garlic," Dr. Levy said. "Eat plenty of apples. Put some blueberries and walnuts on yogurt."

Joan's face looked sick. "The very thought of all those . . ."

Dr. Levy nodded in understanding. "I know. But you need to gain weight."

"How much?" Joan asked.

"At least eight pounds. More would be best."

"We'll stop by the grocery on the way home," John said, concerned.

Joan looked at him. "I am eating, Dr. Levy. It just seems that no matter what I eat, it doesn't stick to me."

Dr. Levy leaned against his desk. "The cancer cells are fighting hard against you, Joan. You need to fight against them harder. Can you do it?"

"She's the Wrecking Ball," John said, looking at the doctor and trying to make Joan smile.

"She's what?"

"The Wrecking Ball, Champion of 1972. She will jab and punch and kick cancer's butt!"

"Kicking's against the rules," Joan said, correcting him.

"If you're fighting cancer," Dr. Levy said, playing along, "you use whatever method of defense you have."

For a reason he can't describe, John shuts off the saw, turns off the lights in the shop, and walks back inside the house. He senses that something isn't right and enters the kitchen from the garage. The lights are off, the kitchen is dark, and he finds Joan lying on the sofa as the kids play together on the floor. He sits next to her on the couch and squeezes her shoulder. "Don't give up."

She is confused. "I thought you were going to work on the table for a while."

"It's close to dinnertime and the lights are off in the kitchen." She looks at him, perplexed. "It's a setback, Joansie. Don't give up. Please." She begins to shake her head. "Today's the day."

"John . . ."

He raises his hand to stop her. "You need to gain weight, and I'm going to the kitchen to make you chicken alfredo with lots of cream."

She reaches for his hand. "You don't know how to make chicken alfredo."

"That's why I'm calling your mom. Alice will be over here like that," he says, snapping his fingers. "The two of us are going to put weight on you." He jumps up and runs from the room, returning in moments with the blue satin boxer's robe she wore on Halloween, and lays it over her. "When dinner's ready I want you to wear this to the table." He kisses her and leaves the room.

John reaches for the phone on the wall in the kitchen and dials the number. He knows that Alice will help him cook one meal, eight, twenty-four, or a hundred and two! Whatever it takes. They'll cook together, and Joan will gain weight and he'll get fat. He'll do it. Whatever it takes.

November 2012

Days have gone by, and Lauren still has not heard from Bud. "He could be out of town," Gloria says, nibbling on a cookie. "Maybe he goes to Florida for the winter."

"Oh, great!" Lauren says, reaching for a cookie from the tray that was left on Gloria's desk. "I hadn't even thought of that."

"Why do you need to find him anyway?" Gloria asks.

"I'm hoping he can help me solve a mystery."

Gloria takes the final bite of her cookie. "Like the

mystery of who keeps leaving these yummy treats in my office?" She reaches for another cookie. "What did the note call these again?"

Lauren reads it. "Truffle cookies." She looks at the cookie in her hand. "So moist."

"I'm afraid I'm going to get fat eating all these treats," Gloria says. She cranes her neck to see if Miriam is in the hallway. "As soon as I say something like that, big-mouth Miriam has something smart to say." She leans in close to Lauren, whispering, "Do you think I'm getting fat?"

"Not yet." Lauren pops the last bite of cookie into her mouth as she leaves Gloria's office.

"Not yet?" Gloria calls after her. She looks at the cookie and wonders if she should finish it. She shrugs, shoving the last bite into her mouth.

Lauren walks into the tutoring room and picks up the reading book she will be going through with Jenson today. At ten, he still struggles with sounding out words. She feels the baby kick and puts her hand on her stomach.

"Everything okay?" Andrea asks, entering the room.

Lauren smiles. "Sure. The baby has been so active recently. Come here."

Andrea steps to her, and Lauren reaches for her hand, placing it on her stomach. "Wow! Football player? Soccer? Maybe doing ballet?"

"Sometimes it feels like all three at once! For some

reason, the baby decides to be very active while I am trying to sleep!"

Jenson bounces into the room and says, "Hey! What's going on?"

"Come here, buddy," Lauren says. She puts his hand on her stomach and his eyes bug out.

"What is that?"

Lauren and Andrea laugh. "That's my baby. Remember when your mom had your baby brother?"

He nods. "I wanted her to have a frog," he says, disappointed.

Lauren rears her head back, laughing. "Grab your book and look over page twenty-two for me. Then we will go through it together." He walks to a cubicle and Lauren turns back to Andrea. "I have a weird question. Do you happen to buy milk from a local farmer?"

"Miss Andrea, am I supposed to be back here with you, or am I supposed to be in the big room playing?" Chyna says, sticking her head inside the room.

"You're supposed to be back here," Andrea says. "I have your books. Come on in." Chyna bounces past Andrea and Lauren to a cubicle and Andrea follows, stopping to look back at Lauren. "I go to the farmer's market every now and then. Why?"

Lauren waves her hand in the air. "No big deal."

TWENTY-THREE

November 1972

John and Alice help Joan to prepare the Thanksgiving meal. Despite their best efforts to make high-fat meals, Joan has gained only three pounds, not enough for Dr. Levy to remove more of her lung. "This meal alone should put on the five extra pounds you need," John says, kissing her cheek.

"This stuffing can do that alone!" Alice says, pouring butter into a bowl with crumbled cornbread, bread, celery, onion, and spices.

"My favorite!" Joan says, reaching into the bowl for a taste. "I haven't had the chance to make it." Her voice carries a hint of sadness, which strikes Alice's heart. "I should have started using your recipes years ago."

"You'll make it," Alice says. She's not talking about the stuffing, and John and Joan both know it. She stops mixing the ingredients together and pushes the bowl in front of Joan. "Today's the day! You make it for Thanksgiving this time, and I'll take over the potatoes." She reaches for the potato that Joan is peeling.

Joan stands quiet, looking at her mom. "Did John tell you to say that?"

Alice looks at John and he shrugs. "Say what? You can make the stuffing?"

Joan looks at John. "'Today's the day.'"

His eyes widen. "I didn't catch that."

Alice is confused, beginning to peel the potato. "What's the big deal about 'today's the day'? It's a pretty common phrase."

Joan begins adding more ingredients to the stuffing. "John says it to me as in 'today's the day God is healing you of cancer.'"

Alice stops peeling and looks up at both of them. "Really?" For as long as Alice has known John, there hasn't been a smack of God talk or about religion or spirituality of any kind from him or Joan, and this surprises her.

"Yeah," Joan says, stopping her work. "What do you think about that?"

Alice is quiet, trying to keep tears from forming, but they rim her eyes anyway. She looks at Joan, smiling. "I think that today's the day!"

November 2012

Lauren is carrying Christmas decorations out of the storage room when her cell phone rings in her pocket. The children are outside, waiting in the pickup line with most of the volunteers. She reaches for her phone, answering it. "Hello."

"Is this Lauren?"

It is a woman's voice that Lauren doesn't recognize. "Yes."

"This is Kathy Waters. You left a note on my father-in-law Bud's door."

"Right!" Lauren says, bubbling with excitement as she reaches with one hand for another small box of decorations.

"I wanted to let you know that he's been in Arizona, visiting his brother, but while he was there Bud became ill and his trip home is delayed until he's better. He hasn't seen your note. Can I help you?"

Lauren continues to pull decorations from the shelves. "I don't know. This is going to sound crazy, but I found a lot of recipes inside a table that I bought, and some of the recipes mention buying milk from Bud. I'm hoping he can remember who these recipes belong to because I don't think their owner meant to give them away with the table."

"Huh," Kathy says. "I don't know if he'd be able to re-member someone or not. My father-in-law is elderly and not in the best physical shape anymore. He sold the farm years ago. My husband flew out this morning to be with him in Arizona. When we're able to bring him home, I will tell him to call you."

"Thanks," Lauren says. "And I hope your father-in-law gets better soon."

"Thanks! I do, too."

Lauren hangs up and realizes she has done everything that she can do to find the owner of the recipes. She hates to think that someone has lost them forever, but there's nothing more she can do. She is opening the boxes of the decorations when Gloria, Miriam, Dalton, Heddy, Amy, Stacy, and Andrea finish with afternoon pickup and step back inside. "Same areas as last year, Gloria?" Lauren asks.

"Whatever you think best," Gloria says.

Each box is marked with the location where the dec-orations were used last year: *front window, entry doors and check-in, bulbs for tree, tutoring room, reading center, Gloria's office,* etc. "All right!" Lauren says. "Grab a box and deco-rate a section. Dalton, can you get the tree out of the stor-age room and carry it to the front entry? We'll have the kids make decorations this week for the tree, but here's a box of bulbs for it."

Gloria reaches for a box. "Come on. We can get this done in thirty minutes or so. Many hands make light work!"

Miriam scoffs. "Hurry up, everyone, before Gloria pelts us with more of her Southern phrases."

Gloria walks across the big room to the reading center. "That's not southern, Miriam."

Miriam picks up a box for the front windows. "If it's not British, it's Southern. Everything American sounds the same to me."

"And everything British sounds goofy," Gloria says, opening a box. "Tiggety who! What does that even mean?"

Miriam pulls decorations from the box in a huff. "It's tickety-boo, Gloria, and I can assure you that things are *not* tickety-boo right now." Gloria laughs and hands her a reindeer decoration for the front window ledge.

Lauren loads a classic Christmas CD into the player and turns it up, drowning out Gloria and Miriam. "Christmas spirit, people!" She puts on an elf hat and wraps tinsel around her neck as she decorates Gloria's office. When she finishes, she walks into the entryway, where Miriam is putting up the final evergreen swags across the wall at the top of the doors. Dalton, Heddy, Gloria, Andrea, and Amy are putting their empty boxes back into the storage room as Lauren turns on the switch for the lights draped over each doorway. "Woo-hoo!" she says, looking at the room. "Just a little Christmas cheer does wonders for a room! Come on! Let's take a picture." They squeeze in together in front of the reindeer cutouts on the wall and smile as Lauren takes a selfie. She raises her arm to take another one but stops, clutching her stomach, bending over.

"Are you okay?" Andrea asks, next to her.

"What is it, babe?" Gloria asks, putting her hand on Lauren's back.

Lauren stands up straight. "I don't know. That was more than a kick. It—" She doubles over again and Dalton steps to her side, wrapping his arm around her waist.

"We need to get you to the doctor," Andrea says.

"I really think I'm fine. Agh!" Lauren says, groaning in pain.

"You're clearly not fine," Miriam says.

"I'll get my car," Andrea says, running for the front doors.

"I'll get your bag out of your locker," Gloria says to Lauren. Lauren groans in pain again, and Miriam helps Dalton get her through the doors and to Andrea's car. Gloria opens Lauren's locker and reaches for her bag, hanging inside. She notices something in the top cubby of the locker, but there isn't time to think about it. It will have to wait until later. She hurries the bag outside and gets into the backseat with Miriam. "We'll call as soon as we hear something," she says, waving to Dalton and Heddy.

TWENTY-FOUR

November 1972

Since Thanksgiving, Alice has been living with Joan and John. When Joan has enough strength, she helps Alice in the kitchen; when she is unable, Alice takes food on a tray to her inside the bedroom or in the living room. "We have to make sure Mommy gains weight," she says to Gigi and Christopher, setting a tray down on Joan's lap with a plate filled with a chicken salad sandwich and a cup of butternut squash soup.

"You still want her to get fat?" Gigi says, sitting on the sofa next to Joan.

Alice smiles. "The doctor wants her to gain weight."

"Dear God, please make Mommy fat," Gigi says into the air as she bounces off the sofa to play with the LEGO bricks that are strewn across the floor with Christopher.

Joan is quiet as she looks at the food. "Mom, I . . ."

Alice sits down next to her. "Just a few bites? Please?"

"I just don't think I can right now. I want to, but . . ."

"You only took one bite of toast this morning." Alice puts her hand on top of Joan's. "Can you try? You're so close, Joan. You can have the surgery and . . ."

"And then what?" Joan is looking at her mom without tears or fear or any worry. "Another surgery?"

"Maybe," Alice says, her voice a mixture of understanding and hope. "Maybe, Joan. We don't know. I know it's a bad day, but this meal could turn it around," she says, smiling.

"How many times did you tell us that when we were kids?" Joan says, grinning. "'Everything will look different once you eat dinner!' Or, 'Come eat these cookies. They'll turn your whole day around!'"

Alice chuckles. "Well, it's true!"

"According to you, anyone who has a bad day just hasn't had a good meal." Joan leans her head onto her mom's shoulder. "I never thought I'd have a hard time eating what you've cooked. You were the best mom." Alice's eyes fill at the words. "You still are."

Alice uses her index finger to dab under each eye. "I didn't come here to blubber. That's not helpful at all. My mission is to fill your stomach with good food and put weight on you!"

"That's my mission, too!" Gigi says from the floor.

Joan chuckles. "So many people on the same mission around here!" She looks at her mom. "Stay with me while I eat?"

Alice lifts Joan's hand and kisses it. "Of course! I love to watch people eat my food!"

November 2012

"What in the world are Braxton Hicks contractions?" Heddy asks inside Gloria's office.

"False labor," Lauren says. She thinks for a moment. "If those were false, what do the real ones feel like?" Gloria, Miriam, Andrea, and Heddy laugh out loud. "Why are you all laughing?"

"You'll laugh someday," Heddy says. "Not at the moment of contractions, though."

"No," Gloria adds. "At that moment you'll want to kill Travis." The women cackle again, making Lauren nervous.

"The doctor, too, for that matter," Miriam says.

"I wanted to break the TV," Andrea says. The women all turn to look at her for an explanation. "I was sitting in a wheelchair while I was being admitted and the news was blaring from a TV set behind me. The most annoying newscaster in the history of news! What I would have given for a baseball bat to bust open that TV and shut that guy's mouth."

Lauren joins them as they laugh, and Gloria puts her arm around her. "We can't wait to hear your story, babe. It really is one of the best days of your life."

As the women leave Gloria's office to head back into the big room, Lauren stops, looking at her. "Gloria? What do you think the percentage is of kids who eat a meal with their parents or whoever has guardianship of them?"

Gloria raises her eyebrows, looking up to the ceiling. "Hmm. I've never thought about that in percentages. Some do. I don't know how many."

Lauren leans against the door. "Do you think any of them cook with their parent or guardian?"

Gloria shakes her head. "I don't know. I imagine that some do. Why?"

"Andrea said something to me a while back and I've been thinking about it. Is it possible to have some sort of cooking class here? You know, small things like how to scramble an egg, how to bake a potato, cook rice, or boil an egg, or how to make cookies. Things I didn't know how to do." Gloria ponders the thought. "I know. It'd be too expensive. We'd need a stove and an oven and a sink and . . ."

Gloria raises her hands in the air. "Hold on! Hold on! I haven't said anything yet." She nods. "Yes, there would be some expense, but we have generous donors."

"But is it a good idea?" Lauren asks, uncertain.

"I like it, and I think it's needed. Who knows how it could inspire one of our kids here?" Lauren smiles. "Let's talk it through with Dalton, Heddy, Miriam, and even Marshall. Let's hear what they think." Lauren begins to leave the office. "Who would teach the classes?"

"Me," Lauren says. "If you'll let me."

TWENTY-FIVE

November 1972

J ohn examines the fourth table leg and sighs. "Finally!
All four legs." The doctor has scheduled Joan's surgery four days from now, firmly believing that her weight
is close enough. Between work, helping with the children,
and grocery shopping, he manages to sneak in an hour or so
of work on the table every few days. He hopes, even prays
that he can have the table finished by Christmas for Joan.
He has taken his family to church for the last two months,
and if Joan is able following her surgery, he envisions taking them to the Christmas Eve service and then coming
home to put Gigi and Christopher to bed. He and Joan
can put the presents beneath the tree and then he can make
sure that she is resting comfortably in bed before he brings
the table inside from the workshop. He can only imagine
Joan's face when she sees it on Christmas morning.

He looks at the pieces of the table and wishes again he could remember the name of the man he met in the hospital cafeteria following Joan's surgery. He would love to talk to him about the table and even more. He would love to talk to him about Joan's surgery, about prayer, about why cancer exists in the first place, and about doubting all that he's learned to believe in the last few months. Even with a few extra pounds, Joan is weak; he knows that, and the surgery scares him. He presses the palms of his hands into his eyes to hold back the tears. In the last several months he has tried to be strong for Joan and his family in every way, but fear spreads across his chest.

Tears fall over his face and he swipes them away. "Don't!" he says to himself. He picks up one of the pieces of wood for the tabletop and examines it. He needs to glue these pieces together. Another tear falls, and John brushes his shoulder against his cheek. "Stop it!" he yells. "Stop!" He throws the tape measure, pencils, and clamps from atop the workbench across the room and slides to the floor. "I'm trying to believe," he whispers. "She's my world. I've loved only her. She's the only one." A knock at the door startles him, and John hurries to his feet. Who would knock? Joan, Alice, or the kids would march right in. He uses the tail of his shirt to wipe his face and hears another knock. He walks to the door and opens it to a man he's never seen before.

"John?" The man is in his late sixties or early seventies, with thinning brownish gray hair and glasses. "When I knocked on your front door, your mother-in-law told me you were out here. I'm Ed Grassle from church. I was told about your wife and wondered if I could come visit with you. Is that okay?"

John feels a lump in his throat and nods. "Sure. Come on in." He leads Ed into the workshop and points at a metal stool. "You're welcome to sit there."

"Maybe in a minute," Ed says, noticing the pieces of wood on the workbench. "Are you making a table? Beautiful wood. Black walnut."

John nods. "Yeah. I started it a few months ago. You know it's black walnut?"

Ed picks up one of the table legs. "I've been dabbling for years. This is beautiful work. You're very talented." John smiles. Ed holds the leg higher, examining it.

"I don't know about that. I spend a lot of time just standing here and staring at the wood, it seems."

Ed smiles. "Then you're a craftsman through and through!" He holds the table leg closer to him and runs his hand up and down it. "Have you ever thought about a piece of wood? Or even a tree, for that matter?"

John looks at him, surprised. "Yeah, I have!"

"Amazing, right? No lab can come up with a tree."

"Or a seed," John adds.

"Or a seed," Ed says, agreeing. He sets the table leg down and looks at John. "There's a lot we can't do, isn't there." He doesn't say it as a question, but rather as more of a statement. Ed knows his place in the universe. "John, when I heard about your wife, I wanted you to know that you're not alone." John bites the inside of his mouth, nodding. "I know you must be awfully scared right now and wondering about what will happen." A tear falls down John's cheek, and he brushes it away. There are people who make you feel instantly at ease and immediately cared for because their words, the way they slip their hands into their pockets, even the way they walk let you know that the only place they want to be right now is with you. This is Ed to John. "You don't know me, but I'll do anything for you and your family. My wife and I both will. We don't want you or your family to feel alone, John." The fear, pain, hurt, stress, and anxiety rush to John's chest, and he wraps his arms around Ed. Ed claps him on the back just like the good father that John imagines him to be, and he stands quietly, letting John cry.

November 2012

Gloria's house is decorated with a mixture of Christmas swags, bulbs, stars, and Nativity sets, with pink, yellow, blue, and green balloons and streamers strung across the ceiling and doorways. Gloria looks around her living room and sighs. "If they came here today, *House Beautiful* would be so confused that they'd never feature me in their magazine."

"I don't think that would be the only reason," Miriam says before clapping her hands together. "All right! Put these cards over there on the gift table. They're for each person to write down some baby advice." Gloria reaches for a pen from the cup on the table and writes: *Don't listen to Miriam* before folding it and setting it inside the basket. "What did you write, Gloria?" Miriam says, her voice dripping with suspicion.

"The best advice Lauren will receive today," Gloria says. "It's something I wish I'd known years ago myself."

There's no time for Miriam to read the card, as guests are at the door, waiting to come inside. "Come, come," Miriam says, ushering them inside. "Gifts over there. Lauren will be here in a few minutes."

Gloria moves to the kitchen and straightens the food on top of the counter. "I still think we should have told Lauren about the shower," she says to Miriam and Heddy.

"She didn't want a shower," Miriam hisses.

"Well, things like this make her uncomfortable," Gloria says, cutting a coconut pie into eight pieces. "We could have brought gifts to her home without the fanfare that makes her squirm."

Miriam scoffs at the thought. "A baby shower will not make her squirm. Whatever you wrote on that card will make her squirm!" The doorbell rings and Miriam shouts, "She's here! Everyone quiet!"

Gloria sticks a finger in the ear that's closest to Miriam's shouting and walks to the front door, opening it. "Hello, babe! Come on in."

Lauren walks inside and jumps at the chorus of voices yelling *"Surprise!"* at her. "So, we're not actually meeting about the fund-raiser?" Lauren asks, smiling as she takes off her coat.

Gloria takes her coat and wraps an arm around her. "We just want you to know that we love you and your baby."

Lauren's eyes get misty and she hugs Gloria, the woman who's more like a mother to her than anyone she's ever known. Miriam steps beside her, and Lauren wraps her arms around her. "You organized this just like you organized my wedding, didn't you, Miriam?" Miriam pats her back and gives Gloria a look that says *I told you so.* Lauren squeezes her in a hug. "Thank you."

After the presents are unwrapped and as Lauren is finishing eating a slice of cake, her cell phone rings. She pulls it out of her back pocket and looks at the number but doesn't recognize it. "Hello."

"Lauren?" An older man's voice shouts on the other end. "This is Bud Waters. I understand you want to talk to me."

Lauren sets down her cake and moves to Gloria's bathroom so she can hear. "Yes! How are you, Mr. Waters? I heard you were sick."

"I was!" he says, shouting. "I got awfully sick in Arizona. I got food poisoning and then it just snowballed from there."

Lauren closes the bathroom door. "I'm so sorry! Are you all better?"

"Getting there every day," Bud says, still at full volume. "How can I help you?"

"I . . ." There's something in his voice that makes Lauren want to meet him face-to-face. "Actually, do you think I could come to your house and talk to you about it? It's about someone who used to buy milk from you. I'm trying to find them."

"Well, if you want to do that, that's fine with me. Do you still have my address? You left a note so I'm assuming you do."

Lauren chuckles. "Yes, I'm all set. Is it okay if I come this afternoon?"

"About what time? I eat my dinner around four thirty," he yells at decibels that Lauren's ears have never heard.

"Will you get here before then? If it's later, do you want me to save you some dinner?"

She laughs out loud. "No, I'll be okay. Thank you, though. I can be there around two o'clock." Lauren opens the bathroom door and smiles.

TWENTY-SIX

December 1972

J ohn sits at the kitchen table and opens Joan's recipe box, pulling out a card and looking at it: *Aunt Dee-Dee's Peanut Butter Fudge.* That was one of the first things Joan made from her mother's recipes. When was that? Six or seven months ago? *Don't even try to skimp on the sugar,* Alice wrote. *It's Christmas, for crying out loud!* John smiles, reading the card.

"What are you doing?"

John jumps at the voice and turns around to see Joan standing in the kitchen doorway leading into the hall. "I was just looking over your aunt DeeDee's recipe for fudge."

"Don't skimp on the sugar," Joan says, stepping toward him.

"It's Christmas, for crying out loud," he adds.

She sits down at the table, reaching for his hand. "Thanks for putting up the Christmas tree this year. Sorry I wasn't much help."

He smiles. "The kids had fun. And you did help. You barked orders at us from the sofa."

She chuckles. "Somebody has to be in charge. Otherwise, it's chaos."

"Things were fine until Christopher got hold of the icicles. That's when chaos broke loose!"

She chuckles, thinking about it. "Who invented icicles anyway?"

"Satan," he says, making her laugh.

Joan points to the recipe card in his hand. "Do you want to make some?"

He looks up at her. "Now?" She nods. "What about your surgery?"

"That's two days from now. I can eat all the peanut butter fudge I want today. We could bring the kids in. It would give them a break from pulling the icicles off the tree." He smiles, looking at her. He knows she's weak and afraid. He knows she doesn't have the energy for it right now. "Today's the day, right?"

He stands up and pulls her to him. "It is."

"And peanut butter fudge makes everything better, right?"

He laughs. "According to your mom, yes!"

December 2012

Lauren knocks loud enough for Bud to be able to hear and smiles when she hears the door unlocking. A tall, thin, elderly man with snow-white hair smiles back at her. "Mr. Waters?"

The door squeaks as he opens it toward her. "Yeah! Call me Bud, Lauren! Come in!" She enters the small living room with a couch and recliner that are long past worn. "Sit down anywhere."

She sits at the end of the sofa and looks around the room; the wall behind the sofa is covered with photos, some of them taken on a farm. "Was this your farm?" she says loud enough for the walls to shake.

He stands in front of the couch, peering at the pictures. "Yep. The farm in Grandon." He pauses for a moment, taking in the picture. "My dad owned it before me."

"It was a family business?"

Bud shakes his head. "Nah. Ended with me. My boys didn't want to farm. Can't blame them. It's not what it once was. It's harder than ever to farm."

"Was it a dairy farm?"

He nods. "The milk that farm produced!" He fades off just thinking about it. "You know, it's not even a farm anymore. Some big shot bought the property and built an enormous house and created pastures for horses. Things change."

Lauren points at one of the pictures. "Is this your family?"

"That's Ron. He and his wife live just a few miles from here. He's an accountant. His kids are grown and spread all over, but they come home when they can. And this picture here is Kevin and his wife, Kathy. You talked to her. He's been a tire salesman for twenty-five years or so. Their two kids stayed close. They don't live too far from here."

"And your wife?" Lauren asks, wondering if she's asked the wrong thing.

Bud points to a picture of him and his wife standing at the Grand Canyon when they both appeared to be in their seventies. "That's Elaine. She died four years ago."

Lauren can see the sadness in his eyes. "I'm so sorry, Mr. Waters. I shouldn't have asked."

"I'm glad you did," he says, sitting on the recliner. "As a matter of fact, I think I would've been offended if you hadn't. I like it when people ask me about her. Everything I have is because Elaine and I worked together. Couldn't have done it without her." Lauren smiles, thinking of Travis. "I can't help but notice that you're about to be a mom."

Lauren puts her hand on her stomach. "I am! I'm due this month."

"I love being a dad. And a grandpa!" he says in a way

that makes Lauren want to cry. "I hope you love being a mom."

"I think I will," she says, nodding.

"Would you like any water or anything to drink?"

"No, thank you. I'm fine."

He settles farther back into the recliner. "You said something about trying to find someone?"

Lauren leans forward, resting her forearms on her knees. "Yes! I bought a table a few months ago and inside a drawer was a huge stack of recipe cards—so many cards that they belong in their own recipe box. All of the recipes are personalized, written from a mother to her daughter. Some of the recipes mention buying milk from Bud. It took me a long time, but I finally found you! Anyway, I don't think those recipes were meant to be given away. I think they got put into that drawer by accident and someone is missing them. I'm hoping that you can help me find the owner."

Bud uses the back of his hand to rub his cheek. "Are there any names on the cards?"

"No."

"The mother never used the daughter's name?"

Lauren shakes her head. "She didn't. But she would buy whole milk from you and make yogurt. She would buy cream and make all sorts of recipes, telling her daughter that fresh milk made for the best recipes."

"Do you know when the recipes were written?"

"Not really. But there's no mention of anything modern. She mentions hayrides at Hurleys' Tree Farm."

"The Hurleys did that thirty or so years ago. I haven't heard of them doing that in recent years."

"So, the cards could be at least thirty years old," Lauren says. "The mother said on the cards that she would pick up her milk on Saturday morning. Do you remember a woman who would come by on Saturdays who talked about cooking at all?"

Bud's face looks disappointed. "I'm sorry. A lot of people came to the farm and my wife or kids dealt with them more than I did."

Lauren realizes something and pulls her phone out of her purse. "I just remembered that I took a picture of some of the cards. Maybe the handwriting will look familiar." She stands up and walks to the recliner, kneeling down next to it and holding the phone so he can see. "On second thought, I should've just brought the cards. That would have made more sense than taking a picture." She accidentally taps the wrong thing on her phone and the photos she took weeks ago from Halloween at Clausen's, decorating at Glory's Place, and from the parks department Christmas party pop up. "Oops. Hold on. I need to scroll down and—"

"Is that Gigi?" Bud asks, looking at a picture on the phone.

"Who?"

He indicates he wants to see a picture she passed and she scrolls back, stopping when he points to a picture. "Gigi. She and her mother Joan used to come here. Whatever happened to them?"

Lauren beams at the picture and leans up, hugging Bud's neck. "You did it!"

"Did what?" Bud asks, surprised.

"You solved the mystery!"

"Well, how'd I do that?"

"By being brilliant," she says, smiling. She stands to her feet. "If I invited you to my house for dinner, would you come?"

"Of course!"

TWENTY-SEVEN

December 2012

"Who can come to our house for dinner on Friday night?" Lauren asks at a meeting inside Gloria's office where Dalton and Heddy, Andrea, Miriam, Amy, and Gloria are discussing the annual fund-raiser taking place in two weeks. "Gloria, feel free to bring Marshall, Andrea, please bring Bill, and Amy, you have to bring Gabe and Maddie."

Dalton and Heddy accept the invitation right away, along with Gloria and Miriam. "That seems like so many people," Andrea says. "Are you sure?"

"The more the merrier," Lauren says. "Larry and his wife are coming, and Robert and Kate Layton and . . ."

"So many people," Gloria says. "What can we all bring?"

"Nothing. Travis and I are taking care of everything. We want to say thank you for all you've done."

"We could at least bring the appetizers," Gloria says.

"Nope. They're covered. Everything's covered," Lauren says, grinning.

On Friday evening, Lauren opens the door and smiles at Bud, who's wearing a bright red sweater and a green knit cap pulled tight over his ears. "You look all Christmassy," she says, moving aside so he can come in. "Bud, this is my husband, Travis."

Travis extends his hand, smiling. "So glad you could come, Bud. Lauren was excited to track you down."

Bud gives a sheepish smile. "Well, I don't know how helpful I was . . ."

"Very," Lauren says, closing the door. "Come on in. Would you like an appetizer? I have a delicious chocolate chip cheeseball with gingersnap cookies and a Vidalia onion dip with tortilla chips." She leads him into the kitchen and hands him a small plate for the appetizers, which she has laid out on the table. "Here's some punch. Or I have tea or water."

"Punch is fine," Bud says. "It's been a long time since I've had punch. My daughter-in-law says it's too sugary and I shouldn't drink it."

Lauren pats Bud on the arm. "It's a special night and I won't tell her." She hands him a small glass of punch. "This is the table I told you about. See, this drawer contained all the recipes."

The doorbell rings, and Travis walks to the front door as Bud stands and admires the table. "And you bought this at a garage sale with the recipes in the drawer?" he asks Lauren.

"No, no. I bought it from a man named Larry who found it at a garage sale years ago. He refinished it."

"Bud?"

Bud and Lauren both turn toward the voice that came from the kitchen doorway. Bud takes a moment looking at the man and pieces memories together. "John?"

Lauren doesn't know this gentleman who looks to be seventy-something. She watches as John walks to Bud and sticks out his hand. "Look at you after all these years. I'm so sorry about Elaine." He glances to the doorway and says, "You remember my daughter . . ."

"Gigi," Bud says, smiling. "Of course."

Lauren smiles. "Gigi?"

"My parents called me Andi," Andrea says, standing next to her husband, Bill. "My brother tried to say Andi but it came out as Angie. Then it morphed into Gigi and it stuck. Like glue. Forever. Until I had kids and then I put my foot down," she says, chuckling.

"I'm so sorry," John says, moving to Lauren. "You must be Lauren! Andrea has spoken so highly of you and said you're about to be parents any day now," he says, smiling at Travis. "Boy or a girl?"

"It's going to be a surprise," Lauren says.

"That's great," John says. "Sorry to be tagging along unexpected. We just drove in today."

"Not at all," Lauren says. "The more the merrier! I told Andrea we have plenty of food."

John smiles. "It's so good to see Bud after all these years!"

"How do *you* know Bud?" Andrea asks Lauren.

"I don't," Lauren says. "I tracked him down."

"Like a bloodhound," Bud says, winking at her.

"Remember that day in the tutoring room when I asked if you bought milk from a local farmer?" Lauren asks. Andrea nods. "I wish I had asked you if you knew a farmer named Bud! That would have solved everything a whole lot quicker!"

"Solved what?" Andrea says, noticing the front door opening. "This is my mom, Joan, by the way." A simple-looking woman in her seventies is carrying a Christmas gift bag as she follows Travis into the kitchen, smiling. "Mom, this is Lauren."

Joan hands the gift bag to her. "I forgot this in the car

and had to get it. We can't drop in like this without bringing you something."

Lauren takes the bag, smiling, as Andrea says, "Mom, you remember Bud Waters."

Joan turns to Bud and her face opens wide in surprise. "Bud Waters! How many years has it been? I still complain that even the organic milk I buy in the store is nothing like what you sold to us." Lauren can barely contain herself watching and listening to them catch up.

"Solved what?" Andrea asks Lauren again.

Lauren looks at Bud, smiling, and waits for a break in their conversation. "Well, I found some things, but I knew the owner would want them back." She steps to the table. "It took me a while, but I hoped Bud could help." Everyone glances at Bud, confused. "I opened my phone at his house, and he happened to see a picture of Andrea, whom he recognized as Gigi." Andrea looks surprised, listening as Lauren opens a drawer under the table. "I think the owner of these is Andrea." She pulls out the recipes as John, Andrea, Bill, and Joan's mouths drop open.

Andrea rushes to grab the recipes from Lauren. "It can't be." She shuffles through them. "Mom! Oh my gosh! Your recipes! Dad! It's your table!" Her eyes fill with tears and she snaps her head to look at Lauren. "Where did you . . . How did you find . . ."

"I bought the table from Larry," Lauren says. "Remember? Miriam went with me and we found it."

"How did Larry have the table?" Andrea asks, sitting down on a chair and running a hand over the tabletop.

"He said he bought it at a garage sale years ago and it was in bad shape. Covered in nail polish, had dings in it and whatever. Said the drawer was sealed shut. It sat in his shop for a couple of years before he refinished it."

Andrea shakes her head in disbelief. "It was all a mistake. Mom and Dad gave me the table right before Bill and I married. Dad knew how much I loved that table and everything it meant." She stops, recalling that difficult time forty years earlier. "He was making this table when Mom was diagnosed with breast cancer that ended up moving to her lungs." Her voice catches and she uses a finger to swipe beneath an eye. "This table inspired Mom to learn how to cook from recipes my grandmother had given her. My brother, Christopher, and I would jump in and help, and then Mom got sick and Dad helped, Grandma helped, and people from Elmore Community Church helped and they didn't even know us!" She looks at Joan and John, remembering. "What a scary, horrible time for my parents, but the love and the help that our family received is unbelievable to this day."

"Your recipes don't mention anything about cancer," Lauren says to Joan.

Joan shakes her head. "No. It was such a huge part of our lives for so long that I didn't want Andrea to look at a recipe and think of the cancer, but rather to think of the person who gave me the recipe. We gathered a lot of recipes from wonderful cooks during that time," she says, smiling.

"But how did the table get lost in the first place?" Travis wonders out loud.

Andrea sighs. "The lid to my recipe box had broken and I put the recipes in the drawer just until I could replace the box. Then we . . ." She looks up at Bill.

"We were moving to a different house," Bill says. "We had a garage sale with some neighbors, and I don't even know how it happened, but somehow the table that was set aside for the move got sold, and Andrea was devastated."

"She cried for days," Joan says.

"Weeks!" John adds.

"Because the table you had made was gone—and all of Mom's recipes!" Andrea says, running her hand again over the top of the table.

"Larry thinks it was probably used for children," Lauren says. "And they probably never bothered to try to open the drawer once they managed to seal it shut. He said he couldn't open it at all and had to work away at it, which is the only explanation for why the recipes were still in there."

Joan sits at the table across from Andrea. "I can't believe it. I haven't seen the table in years," she says, her hands tracing the edge of it. "Oh, my goodness, John." She glances up at him. "All those months of making this." She looks at Lauren. "What in the world made you track down the owner of those recipes?"

Lauren smiles, leaning into Travis. "It's going to sound weird, but I just knew that whoever wrote those recipes really loved her daughter and there was no way that daughter would willingly give them away. And in another weird way, I felt close to all of you. I wanted to learn to cook because of the recipes, and Travis and I have cooked a lot of things together. I actually think I'm a pretty good cook now," she says, laughing.

"You never know what's going to happen in life, do you?" Joan says.

TWENTY-EIGHT

December 2012

The doorbell rings, and Travis walks to the front hall-way and opens it. "Hey, Travis!" Lauren can hear Larry's voice on the front porch. "Gloria needed these for the fund-raiser, and I was passing by, so I thought I'd drop them off."

"Come on in," Travis says. He takes two wooden keep-sake boxes from Larry, setting them down on a side table in the living room.

"I'm sorry," Larry says. "I didn't know you had company."

"No!" Lauren says. "Larry, come in! This is perfect." She looks at Joan and John. "This is Larry, the man who refinished the table. Larry, this is John and he made this table back in . . ." She realizes she doesn't know when John made the table and stops.

"In 1972," John says, looking at Larry. He steps to him and sticks out his hand. "John Creighton."

"Nice to meet you, John," Larry says, shaking his hand.

"And you're Larry." John stops, looking at Larry's face. "Larry! Larry from the hospital."

"Just Larry from Grandon," Larry says. He pauses for several moments before his mouth turns up in a grin of realization. "John?" he says, whispering. "John from the hospital!" The men pump each other's hands before embracing and laughing together.

"Joan! This is Larry. Remember after your first surgery I told you I met him in the cafeteria."

Joan's eyes get misty looking at him. "The man who taught John how to pray."

Larry shakes his head. "No, I just talked about wood."

"No," Joan says. "John changed after he met you. God put you there for him that day." Larry begins to shake his head. "He did! John didn't believe anything at that time. Neither did I. But you were there, and you said what John needed. Christmas became new to us because of you! You set John on a journey to discover who God and His Son are." She steps to him and hugs Larry. "Just like a woman named Ronnie was there in the chemo room one day with her son and she said what I needed. Just like a man named Ed from church showed up at John's workshop door at the time he needed him. And just like you had this table when Lauren needed one. God doesn't waste any opportunities. We do." She turns to look at Lauren. "I'm so glad you didn't waste this opportunity." She hugs Lauren, and Lauren beams from ear to ear.

"These," Lauren says, picking up the rest of the recipes on the table and handing them to Andrea, "belong to you. I hope you don't mind, but I made a copy of each one of them."

"I made her," Travis says. "Hope we didn't infringe on any copyright laws." Andrea laughs, shaking her head.

"And the table is yours, too," Lauren says.

"I can't take the table," Andrea says. "You bought it."

"It's yours," Lauren says. "It belongs in your family for as long as possible."

"I'll make you a new one," John says to Lauren.

"*We* can make you a new one," Larry pipes in, winking at John. "Do you still work with wood, John?"

"I still dabble."

"He doesn't dabble," Joan says. "He makes beautiful things."

"Don't tell me you live in Grandon and we've not seen each other all these years?" Larry asks.

"We never lived in Grandon," John says. "Just over the line in Elmore."

"And we met at City Hospital twenty miles from each

one of us," Larry says, amazed. "When was that?" He searches his brain for the answer. "Forty years ago!" Larry looks at Joan. "You had part of your lung removed."

Joan nods. "And then later I had more of it removed. And it was a long recovery, but it seems the entire community rallied around us. Elaine would bring me milk," she says, looking at Bud.

"I remember that," Bud says.

"And she never charged me a dime for all that milk and cream she dropped off."

"Oh, I didn't know that," Bud says, making everyone laugh.

"She's been cancer-free as long as I've been in the family," Bill says.

"She was a wrecking ball against cancer," Andrea says. "She and Dad both were. They were a team. Mom even has the robe to prove it." Joan laughs, thinking about that silly robe from Halloween that still hangs in her closet.

"Who's ready to eat?" Lauren says.

Andrea looks out the kitchen window to the driveway. "What about Gloria and Marshall, Miriam, Dalton and—"

"Oh! They weren't really invited," Lauren says, grinning. "I told them before the meeting that day that I had a surprise for you and needed all of them to agree to come here just so you'd come. I even made up Robert and Kate Layton to make it sound like a party. I couldn't believe it when you called today and said your parents had driven into town and asked if it would be okay to bring them! This turned out better than I ever imagined!"

"I feel like a party crasher," Larry says sheepishly.

"You have *made* the party!" Lauren says, opening her arms wide and running to him to give him a hug. "You were definitely meant to be here!"

Lauren passes out punch to those who don't have any and raises her glass. "To a table that brought us all together!"

"And to beating cancer," Andrea says.

"And to wood!" Larry adds, looking at John.

"And hospital cafeterias," Joan says.

"And to dairy farmers," John says.

"And to handwritten family recipes," Bud says, laughing.

"And to old friends and family memories," Bill says.

"And to babies who are about to be born," Travis says, putting his arm around Lauren.

"And to mysteries that are solved," Lauren shouts as they clink their glasses together.

TWENTY-NINE

December 2012

Lauren works alongside Miriam as they set silent auction items onto tables near the gazebo for the annual Glory's Place fund-raiser. Nearby, Travis, Dalton, Gabe, and Amy set up chairs. In just a few hours the children from Glory's Place will be performing Christmas songs and carols for what they hope will be their most successful fund-raiser ever. "Whose idea was it to start having this fund-raiser outside in December?" Miriam sneers.

"Uh, it was mine," Lauren says, grinning.

Miriam stops her work, looking at Lauren. "Oh, that's right. If you weren't pregnant, I'd say something, but I won't for fear the baby will hear and won't like me."

Lauren laughs out loud and grips her stomach. "Miriam!"

Miriam runs around the table to her side and sees that Lauren's water has broken. "Now I've done it! Me and my big mouth!"

Lauren grabs her hand, squeezing it. "Miriam! Get Travis!"

"Of course!" She turns to yell for Travis but looks back at Lauren. "I really don't mind the fund-raiser being out here. It's actually quite fun, but I could never let Gloria know that, you know. And I certainly don't blame you for—"

"Miriam!"

Miriam jumps, turning again to run toward Travis. "Travis!" she says, running to where he is unloading more chairs from the back of a truck parked near the gazebo. "Travis! The baby is coming!"

"What?" Gloria says, snapping her head up from a conversation with Betty Grimshaw from Betty's Bakery about a delivery of baked goods this afternoon. "Everybody get out of the way!"

"Nobody's in the way, Gloria," Miriam says, running back to Lauren.

Travis reaches Lauren's side and puts his arm around her waist. "I've got you. The baby's really coming," he says, breathless and smiling.

"The baby's cooomiiing," Lauren says, her face grimacing in pain.

Andrea and her husband, Bill, honk as they pull up to a spot near the gazebo. As they get out of the car to begin helping at the fund-raiser, they stop when they see both Gloria and Miriam waving their arms like air traffic controllers. "Get back in the car!" Gloria yells. "Take Lauren to the hospital!"

Andrea sees Travis and Dalton helping Lauren across the town square, and she runs to the back car door, opening it. "Come on!" she says, waving them on.

The entire setup crew of Gloria, Miriam, Amy, Gabe, Stacy and her son, Ben, and Heddy rush to the car to help Lauren inside. "Gloria, I'm so sorry . . ." Lauren screams again as Travis helps her into the car.

"Sorry nothing!" Gloria says. "We've got everything under control here. We love you, babe! Andrea, call us as soon as the baby comes!"

And with that, Bill backs out of the parking space and heads for the hospital.

"The baby is coming early," Gloria says, watching the car. She turns to look at Miriam, scowling. "What did you do?"

Gloria, Miriam, Dalton, Heddy, Gabe, Amy, and their daughter Maddie, and Stacy and her son, Ben, hurry through the hospital hallway, leading to the maternity ward. Andrea and Bill are waiting at the nurses' station in the middle of the ward. "How's Lauren?" Gloria says, rushing to her.

"She's doing great!" Andrea says.

"A baby girl!" Gloria squeals, clapping her hands together. She realizes how loud she is and shushes herself, putting her index fingers to her lips in front of the nurses. "I'm so sorry! I'm just a proud grandmother who can't wait to see her grandchild!"

"Whatever her name is," Miriam says drily, looking at Andrea. "I don't understand why you couldn't tell us the baby's name."

Andrea holds her hands out in front of her in a shrug. "I don't know the baby's name! She wanted to wait until all of you got here."

"Oh, come on!" Gloria says, tugging on Miriam's arm. "No time to squabble! Take us to our granddaughter!"

Andrea and Bill lead all of them to a room at the end of the hall, where Lauren is propped up on the bed, holding a bundle of pink in her arms. "Theerre sheee iiss," Gloria says, drawing out each word in a high-pitched drawl. "Have you ever seen a child so beautiful?" she asks the group, all craning their necks to see.

"Her face is kind of blotchy!" Maddie says, making everyone laugh, and Gabe puts his hand over her mouth.

"The doctor said that won't last long," Lauren says, grinning at Maddie. "Somebody tell me how the fundraiser went!"

Gloria scoffs. "We will not say a word until you tell us this angel's name."

Lauren holds the baby tighter. "Not until you tell me how it went."

"We raised more money than any other year, thanks to Ben's great idea!" Stacy says. Ben looks sheepish, smiling.

"What idea?" Lauren asks, looking up at Ben.

"For ten dollars, people could guess if you were having a boy or a girl," Stacy says. "We raised an extra $2,600!"

"But most people thought you'd have a boy," Ben says, a bit disappointed.

"But they'll be delighted to meet . . ." Gloria says, hinting that she wants to know the name of the baby.

"Glory," Lauren says, beaming.

Gloria's mouth drops open and Miriam gasps. "Glory?" Miriam says, confounded. "This sweet child has to go through life with the name Glory?"

"Actually, it's Gloria Miriam. We'll call her Glory," Travis says, sitting on the edge of the bed.

Tears fill both Gloria's and Miriam's eyes. "I bet you

don't have anything to say now, do you?" Gloria says to Miriam.

"Oh, be quiet, Grandma," Miriam says, serenely defeated. "A child named after us! I never would have imagined. A perfectly beautiful baby girl." She sighs in happiness. "Gloria Miriam! Welcome to Grandon, little one."

"And while you're home with little Glory, we will be installing an oven, a sink, and a few cupboards," Gloria says. Lauren looks up at her, surprised. "I told you we had generous donors. You can start that cooking class when the time is right."

"I can't believe it," Lauren says.

"I can't believe that we're not going to have more of those delicious treats you were secretly delivering," Gloria says, winking.

"Gloria!" Lauren says. "How'd you know it was me?"

Gloria smiles. "Well, you asked about starting a cooking class, for one thing. And then I saw a plate full of cookies in your locker when I got your purse, that day you had the false labor."

Lauren looks at the faces around her. "Did you all know?"

"Not at first," Miriam says. "But eventually we all figured it out. We just didn't dare say anything because we wanted the treats to keep coming!"

Lauren throws an arm over her face, laughing, as Glory opens her mouth in a yawn.

"Look at that little lamb," Gloria says. She strokes her cheek with the back of her finger. "What a Christmas! Glory, Glory, hallelujah!"

THIRTY

Christmas Day 2012

The sound of Glory's cooing awakens Lauren and she looks over at Travis, who's opening his eyes. "It's her first Christmas," Lauren says, smiling. She flings the blankets and comforter off, racing Travis to get to Glory first. They run to the crib inside the nursery and look down at the little life wiggling and whimpering on her stomach, and Lauren lifts Glory into her arms. "Merry Christmas, my sweet angel," she says, kissing her face.

Travis bends to kiss Glory's cheek and squeezes her hand. "Best Christmas present ever," he says, kissing her tiny hand over and over. "Are you ready to see your presents?" They look at Glory, who stretches her arms over her head, and laugh. "The excitement is overwhelming her," Travis says as he taps the baby's nose. "I can call my parents and tell them we're up."

Lauren nods. "I'll get some coffee on."

Travis returns to their bedroom for his cell phone as Lauren walks downstairs with Glory. "Travis! Hurry!"

He bounds down the stairs to the kitchen, where he sees Lauren standing by a round, black walnut table wrapped in an enormous red bow. Lauren reaches for the card and reads it aloud. "For Christmas breakfast and all other meals that will follow. Merry Christmas, Larry and Meredith and John and Joan."

Christmas 1972

Joan opens her eyes and looks at the clock on her night-stand: 7:30 A.M. "Oh my gosh!" she says, realizing that John is not in bed and that Gigi has probably been awake for two hours, waiting to open presents. She wraps her robe around her and races through the hallway, saying, "I'm so sorry I slept so late!" She stops inside the living room, seeing John, her mom and dad, Gigi, and Christopher standing like guards in front of the Christmas tree.

"Merry Christmas!" Gigi yells as they all break rank, revealing the table that John has been working on for the last several months.

Her eyes fill at the sight of it. "I thought you were behind on the work," she says, looking at John as she reaches out to touch it.

"Ed helped me. I wouldn't have been able to finish it without him."

Joan bends over, examining the table. "It's just beautiful, John."

"A lot of family meals will be eaten around this table," Alice says.

"It's my best present ever," Joan says, kissing John. "Thank you."

"Look, Mommy!" Gigi says, pulling open the drawer underneath. "My favorite part!"

"Oh, this is wonderful!" Joan says. "What could we put inside here?"

"Candy," Gigi says with great Christmas cheer. "Can we open our presents now?"

As they sit down to breakfast around the new table that morning, Joan wonders if she will always remember the laughter and warmth and heart of this day. She wonders if she'll remember the look in John's eyes as he reaches for her hand to squeeze it during grace or if she'll recollect her mom and dad's voices or the squeals of delight from Gigi and Christopher as they marvel in the wonder of the day. She wonders if she'll recount her gratefulness or feel more love for her family than she does on this day, and the answer is yes, she will. She most definitely will.

A Christmas Table Full of Recipes

✵

There isn't room for all of them, but these are some of the recipes that Joan, Lauren, or Alice made, plus longtime family favorites of ours that I pull out during the Christmas season. I use Einkorn all-purpose flour for the baked goods here but your favorite all-purpose will do and I always reduce the sugar at least by half, but experiment according to your taste. That is part of the joy of cooking! Merry Christmas!

AUNT DEEDEE'S
PEANUT BUTTER FUDGE

This recipe was given to us by my husband's great-aunt Dee-Dee Macdonald. It's sweet . . . so sweet it might set your teeth on edge, but you can't stop at one piece, and it is Christmas, after all!

2 cups sugar
⅔ cup milk

1 cup Marshmallow Fluff
1 cup peanut butter
1 teaspoon vanilla

Put the sugar and the milk in a saucepan and cook to soft ball. Take off heat and add the Marshmallow Fluff, the peanut butter, and the vanilla. Stir. Spread the mixture into a 9 x 11 baking dish. Let cool. Cut into pieces to serve.

CHOCOLATE CHIP CHEESEBALL

This is not the typical cheeseball. It's great to take to gatherings or to serve if you're hosting a Christmas party.

1¼ cups roasted, chopped pecans
3 8-ounce packages cream cheese, softened
1½ cups mini chocolate chips
1 cup sifted powdered sugar
1 tablespoon ground cinnamon

Roast whole pecans on a baking sheet in a 350°F oven for ten to twelve minutes. Chop the pecans and set aside. Mix together the cream cheese, the chocolate chips, the powdered sugar, and the cinnamon and form the mixture into a ball. Press the pecans around the entire ball. Chill for several hours. Serve with gingersnaps. So yummy!

SHORTBREAD COOKIES

———————

These are the best shortbread cookies I've ever made, and they have only four ingredients. My friend Val Clemente gave me this recipe, and I always quadruple it for my family because the cookies store very well. I can't tell you how long they keep, though, because we eat them too fast!

　　1½ cups all-purpose flour
　　½ teaspoon salt
　　⅔ cup butter, softened
　　½ cup powdered sugar

Preheat the oven to 325°F. Mix all the ingredients together and roll the dough out on a lightly floured surface to about a quarter inch thick. Cut out cookies with a two-inch cutter and put them on an ungreased cookie sheet. Bake the cookies in the oven for twenty to twenty-five minutes or until they are brown around the edges. Will yield approximately one dozen cookies.

TRUFFLE COOKIES

———————

My mom had a friend who used to say about what she was eating, "This will make you want to smack your mama!" Well, these cookies are so tender they'll make you want to smack your mama! But I don't recommend that. Be kind to your mama.

4 squares (1 ounce each) unsweetened chocolate
2 cups semisweet chocolate chips, divided
⅓ cup butter
¾ cup sugar
3 eggs
1½ teaspoons vanilla extract
½ cup all-purpose flour
2 tablespoons cocoa
¼ teaspoon baking powder
¼ teaspoon salt
Powdered sugar to sprinkle on top

Preheat the oven to 350°F. Melt the unsweetened chocolate, one cup of the chocolate chips, and the butter in a double boiler or in the microwave. Let the mixture cool ten minutes.

Beat the sugar and the eggs for two minutes in a mixing bowl. Beat in the vanilla and the cooled chocolate mixture.

In a separate bowl, combine the flour, cocoa, baking powder, and salt and then beat into the chocolate mixture. Stir in remaining chocolate chips. Cover the mixture and chill it for an hour or so.

Once it has chilled, roll the dough into one-inch balls (you may need to lightly flour your hands) and place them on an ungreased baking sheet. Bake the cookies for nine to twelve minutes or until they are lightly puffed. Cool the cookies on a wire rack. Once they have completely cooled, sprinkle powdered sugar on top. Will yield about three dozen cookies.

THREE-CHEESE EGG CASSEROLE

―――――――――

Guests rave about this casserole every time I make it because it's tender and delicious. For ease, it can be prepared in advance and refrigerated overnight.

7 eggs
1 cup milk
1 teaspoon sugar
1 cup Monterey Jack or Gruyère cheese, shredded
1 to 3 ounces cream cheese, cubed
1 cup small-curd cottage cheese

7 tablespoons butter, melted
½ cup all-purpose flour
1 teaspoon baking powder

Preheat oven to 350°F. Beat together the eggs, milk, and sugar. Add all three cheeses and melted butter and mix well. Mix in the flour and the baking powder. Pour the mixture into a greased three-quart casserole dish.

Bake forty to forty-five minutes or until the casserole is firm and lightly brown on top. If baking directly from the refrigerator it will take closer to an hour to cook through.

PUMPKIN RICOTTA PANCAKES

This is a nice, heavy pancake with the flavors of fall. You can easily add ground flax for additional nutrients. Unlike some pancakes, these stick with you!

1½ cups all-purpose flour
1 teaspoon baking powder
½ teaspoon salt
1 teaspoon pumpkin pie spice
1 tablespoon sugar

2 tablespoons vegetable or coconut oil, melted
1 large egg
½ cup whole-milk ricotta cheese
½ cup plus 2 tablespoons canned pumpkin
½ to ⅔ cup milk (you may need more or less, depending on
how thick your batter is)
White chocolate chips (optional)

Combine the flour, baking powder, salt, pumpkin pie spice, and sugar in one bowl. In a separate, larger bowl whisk together the oil, the egg, the ricotta cheese, and the canned pumpkin. Pour half of the dry ingredients into the wet mixture and whisk. Add a half cup of milk and stir, then add the rest of the dry ingredients and stir to combine. If the batter is really thick, add a little more milk till it reaches the desired consistency. If the batter is thick the pancakes will be thick; a thinner batter will produce a thinner pancake. Spoon the batter onto a lightly buttered griddle set on medium heat. If desired, add a few white chocolate chips on top of each. When several bubbles appear on the top of the pancake, flip it to the other side to continue cooking. Serve with warm maple syrup. Feeds five hungry eaters or six polite ones.

CINNAMON BREAD

We tried a loaf of cinnamon bread at Dollywood in Pigeon Forge, Tennessee, once and have been hooked ever since. It is a buttery, sugary confection that truly is for a special occasion like Christmas breakfast. I make dough for dinner rolls and use that dough in this recipe, but if you don't have homemade yeast dough on hand, it may be easier to buy frozen bread dough. Either way, it's delicious! I don't know if this is Dollywood's exact recipe, but it's pretty darn close!

BREAD

    1-pound loaf of frozen bread dough

    ½ cup sugar

    1½ tablespoons cinnamon

    5 tablespoons butter, melted

    1 cup of roasted pecans broken into pieces (optional)

GLAZE

    1 cup powdered sugar

    1 tablespoon butter, softened

    ½ teaspoon vanilla

    ½ tablespoon milk or orange juice (optional)

Preheat the oven to 300°F. Coat two 8½-inch loaf pans with vegetable oil or butter. Combine the cinnamon and sugar on a plate or a baking mat and set aside. Cut the bread dough lengthwise into two pieces and then make four crosswise slits across the top of each. Don't cut all the way through, but do cut deep enough for the cinnamon sugar to get pretty far down. Brush both loaves with butter, making sure you get deep into the cuts. Roll each loaf in the sugar mixture and pat it into the creases. If desired, cover each loaf with a half cup of roasted pecan pieces. Put each loaf in a bread pan and cover with a dish towel. Set it in a warm place to rise for thirty minutes. Bake the bread for thirty-five minutes or until it's nice and golden on the top, turning the pans once in the middle of the baking time. Remove the bread from the pans.

To make the glaze, mix the first three ingredients until smooth. Add the milk or orange juice if needed. Since not everyone may like glaze, each person can drizzle the glaze over the top of their piece, but if you know that everybody likes it, drizzle away while the loaves are nice and warm! These are best eaten on the same day. Makes two loaves.

TOFFEE POPCORN WITH
CHOCOLATE DRIZZLE

———————

This is yummy for family movie night. Unfortunately, it's hard to stop eating!

32 cups plain popped popcorn (approximately 1 cup of popcorn kernels will yield 32 cups of popped popcorn)
2½ cups brown sugar
1½ cups butter
½ cup light corn syrup
1 teaspoon salt
1 tablespoon vanilla
1 teaspoon baking soda
2 cups bittersweet chocolate chips
Coarse-grain sea salt (optional)

Preheat the oven to 225°F. Pop the popcorn and remove any unpopped kernels. Put the popcorn into a large roasting pan and set aside. (If you have a roasting pan that can fit a turkey, it will have room to spare for 32 cups of popcorn. If you have a small roasting pan, you may need to use an additional 9 × 13 pan.) Combine the brown sugar, the butter, the corn syrup, and the salt in a saucepan. Cook over medium heat and stir occasionally for eight to ten minutes or until the mixture comes to a full boil. Continue cooking for five minutes more. Remove the saucepan from the heat and stir in the vanilla and baking soda. Pour the hot sugar mixture over the popcorn in the roasting pan and stir until well coated. Bake one hour, stirring every fifteen minutes, or until there is a crispy coating on the popcorn. Spread out the popcorn on parchment paper and cool. Microwave the bittersweet chocolate chips, stirring every thirty seconds until they have melted. Drizzle over the cooled popcorn. If desired, sprinkle with coarse-grain sea salt. Let stand until drizzle is firm. Store leftovers in an airtight container. Makes two gallons of toffee corn.

Special Thanks

Special thanks to Troy, Gracie, Kate, and David, who are always up for me trying new recipes, and to Jen Enderlin and everyone at St. Martin's who continue to believe in the power of story, especially at Christmas. And many thanks to my mom, Alice Payne, who passed on the love for a good recipe and taught me how to cook.